PAGES *from the* TEXTBOOK
of ALTERNATE HISTORY

PAGES *from the* TEXTBOOK *of* ALTERNATE HISTORY

Phong Nguyen

Queen's Ferry Press

Queen's Ferry Press
8622 Naomi Street
Plano, TX 75024
www.queensferrypress.com

The characters and events in this book are fictitious. Any similarity to real persons, living or dead, is fully intended by the author, but should be regarded as a fictional version of the past, and not as an objective or nonfictional rendering of history.

Copyright © 2014 by Phong Nguyen

All rights reserved, except for brief quotations in critical articles or reviews. No part of this book may be reproduced in any manner without prior permission from the publisher: Queen's Ferry Press—8622 Naomi Street, Plano, TX 75024

Published 2014 by Queen's Ferry Press

Cover design by Sarah Nguyen

First edition January 2014

ISBN 978-1-938466-23-6

Printed in the United States of America

for David Benjamin Saunders, who carried the fire

Who has grief and who has sorrow?

Who has a thousand years of woe?

— Impossible to sleep

with the roaring crowds of the elected

They pound on the gate

The glass of air shatters

Seconds pour out

and History phosphoresces

...

History phosphoresces, through the loopholes

you can see

statues of mustard, statues of tears

Pounding on the gate,

crying: *History is made by evil men.*

—Sylva Fischerová, "Who Makes History"

translated from the Czech by the author and Stuart Friebert

TABLE *of* CONTENTS

Introduction *11*

The Great Pyre of Egypt *25*

Siddhartha Remains in His Father's Palace *41*

Plato, King of Syracuse *57*

Jesus, Unforsaken *77*

Joan of Arc, Patron Saint of Mothers and Soldiers *93*

Columbus Discovers Asia *115*

John Smith is Hanged for Treason *125*

Ben Franklin, Clergyman *135*

Napoleon Invades Louisiana *159*

Hitler Goes to Art School *177*

Ho Chi Minh in Harlem *195*

Einstein Saves Hiroshima *215*

Epilogue: The Coronation of King George *235*

Introduction

THE TEXTBOOK WAS AN ACCIDENT, a payday gone wrong, its discovery technically illegal, but now that it is *out there*, history compels me to give an accounting of how it came into my hands.

The last chapter, you may already know, was written on the walls. But since this volume will be the first selection of the Textbook in print, I resolved to treat this strange phenomenon as the cultural touchstone that it will inevitably become when all the silicon is used up and we strive to remember what things were like when we wrote on the pulp of trees.

So the history of the alternate history is this:

I never met Obediah Lister or saw him in person. There is an unspoken arrangement at The Workshop that techs do not roam into the storefront where the customers drop off and pick up their machines. But from what Linda told me, Obie had the appearance of a man who has calculated not to draw any attention to himself—graying hair and half-dark glasses, thick eyebrows and a slight paunch overhanging his belt, the pinched facial creases of every other middle-aged man. He slouched forward, she said, like a defeated athlete.

There was nothing distinctive about him at all, Linda said, from behind her desk and her mascara. *Forget him.*

But I could not forget Obediah Lister, like a man who is told not to think of an elephant, who cannot banish the thought of an elephant from his mind.

—

Around that time I would end up at The Workshop every night around 2 A.M. because I couldn't sleep. This surprisingly cold morning in Houston was no different. I stirred, loosening the straps of my mask, and switched off the CPAP; then I took the elevator to the desolate parking garage, where I rode my nearly new hybrid to The Workshop, a ground-floor office bordered by LED screens and windowless fluorescence. I stooped in the low doorway at the bottom of the stairs to avoid dislodging the cork ceiling tiles, and went to work. There is nothing soothing about a room full of glowing rectangles; it was just a place that I steered toward out of habit.

Most of the data-recovery work that week was mechanical. I donned my gloves and opened up the ruined drive that I had been procrastinating over for a week, since it seemed beyond salvation. The circuit board was in bad shape—worn down, bubbling on every circuit. The only reason to suspect it could be recovered at all was that the CPU successfully read the drive as a "USB Device," which meant at least it knew that *something* had been plugged in. It had been propped against the metal tray marked "Tasks," staring at me with its one magnetic eye, ever since. But at that hour between blue night and gray morning, I was full of apprehension.

The circuit board exposed, a fine dark substance encrusted the chips, some pieces flaking off like ash. It was as though the whole board had been submerged in salt water for weeks, then left in the open air to mold. Except there was a sort of space-age bubble raised over one set of circuits, slightly off-center, giving it the unlikely appearance of a wrecked toy spaceship. How could a circuit board possibly get into this condition? And what, dear god, must be contained on this hideous relic? I spent the rest of that night tinkering with the drive, abandoning my usual algorithms, relying on trial and error—an approach to which I hadn't needed to make recourse since I was a cub hacker, cracking open my first Commodore. It was a blissful seven hours I spent reshaping the topography of those once-shiny circuits, now glowing faintly like yellowed teeth. There is a reckless joy in undertaking what seems impossible.

Only when I displaced the raised section of the board that contained the bubble-encased circuits—quite accidentally, while the drive was still plugged in—did the menu item marked "USB Device" on my monitor suddenly load up with the unusual designation "HIC_SVNT_LEONES." What I first took as a random string of letters spewed from the deep code of the machine—strangely, without symbols and numbers—I later learned spelled the unpronounceable syllables of a dead language that warned: Lions_dwell_here.

—

There were no family pictures or personal information in the data we recovered that I could use to create a picture of Obie's interior life, no titillating memoirs or dream journals; but no emails to old flames either, or hastily composed to-do lists, or revealing fetishes.

Instead, Obediah had a terabyte full of images and text—more than two billion words, with half a million maps and timelines—of meticulously organized and scrupulously annotated chapters from a digital textbook so vast that it could only exist in the theoretical dimension: as bits of data appearing one page at a time on the screen, complete with notes, figures, and discussion questions. I ascertained its contents—volume after volume of every conceivable version of historical event, from the first recorded cuneiform script ever written on clay tablet to the last cursor guided by bluetooth-linked keyboard— painstakingly photographed, transcribed and translated, whenever necessary, into American English, but unindexed and unwritable onto any other disk, its data hopelessly scrambled by the rot of old metal sloughing off from the green board like necrotic flesh.

At my work station I had a car seat installed rather than a standard swivel chair, because driving soothed me, and the anonymity of my work allowed for such indulgences. (My desktop image showed the cockpit of a Mercedes, steering wheel in the foreground, a typical red-orange southwestern vista beyond it, the gunmetal gray road tapering into nothing.) So I buckled myself in and began to archive this colossal mess of data. Having just conquered the near-impossible task of fixing an unfixable hard drive, I found myself now shouldering the burden of sorting an unsortable body of text.

No scholar is fit for this work. It wanted that unhealthy

blend of sedentary daily habit and screen obsession that only a hardware geek can summon. It wanted an engineer to take the drooling river and make a dam to fill the basin. It wanted a champion of patience, one who never slept, who could click a mouse eternally if he had to.

The Textbook would be impossible to read within a lifetime, so how could a single man have *written* it? And from where did all these images, these references, this entire body of work, come—if not from some existence parallel to but separate from ours? As soon as I raised this question, its inevitable answer revealed itself. *Nowhere else.* It could only be the product of a hundred thousand civilizations in simultaneous and divergent movement, each potential reality only joined to the next through traces of the written word, fraily encoded in the rotting vessel rapidly degrading in front of me.

More than five times the capacity of Wikipedia, more than sixty times the size of the Britannica, the Textbook could scarcely be read by a single reader, and from this faulty chip it could never be transferred to a more stable drive; yet it could be indexed and archived. The annotations alone could have swallowed up the twenty-one volumes of the OED. But the programming mind had its answer: with a single line of code, the machine organized chapters by date, then culled all chapters that cross-referenced historical personages from other bodies of text that I'd inputted from crowdsourced encyclopedias like the aforementioned, then culled from the yield all the chapters referring to momentous events in *our own* historical timeline, then culled from *those* chapters any that cited books within the Library of Congress database. Within these parameters, I was able to narrow it down to a few thousand pages. Thus began the manual indexing—six red-eyed nights at The Workshop, curating the arcane subject matter of worlds-not-ours.

When I finished indexing the data, on an innocent Thursday morning, ready at last to let the mysterious drive leave my hands, I crossed to the front room, telling Linda that I wanted to contact Obediah directly, a request which she promptly denied. "Why are you up here, anyway?" she said. Better that the customer fix his imagination on whatever version of high-tech genius suits him, she said, than to see the specific face and body of a mere man, with a coffee-stained sweatshirt and loose bags under his eyes. Let his inner vision of the man-behind-the-wall suffice. If it were up to her, all our customers would believe that computers are run by voodoo, and that the-man-behind-the-wall is the only exorcist in town.

—

The next night I got up shortly after midnight, as usual, but this time my heart knocked against the walls of my ribcage like a man in a straightjacket, my forehead freckled with sweat. I was shaken by a sudden fear that the Textbook had been degaussed by a magnetized blimp that quietly passed over the city at night.

At The Workshop, my sense of relief was delayed by an excruciating load time, but seeing the Textbook pop up on the screen gave me brief reassurance. Fresh as I was from this anxiety dream, I immediately sent the files to our print queue for a selected 5, 000 pages. I loaded enough reams into our high-volume printer to last, I thought, the first hour; then I lay down in the breakroom for an overdue nap.

When I awoke, the printer had spat out more than 1, 300 pages, all blank. The drive could not communicate with the printer. I began taking screen shots one at a time and sending each to the printer—tedious, repetitive work; the kind of work that, for a tech, cuts the legs out from under you. At that moment, the power shut off and I was left in the orange glow of the security lights, with no emanating LED screens. Panicking, thinking only of what I might have lost, I took a ream of paper and a fresh supply of Bics and began to frantically copy what little I remembered from the fading impressions on the dark screen. By opening hour Monday, I had two hundred pages, scribbled on copy paper and spread chaotically around my work station.

That morning Linda found me cheek-down on the keyboard. Stirring me with a shake, she told me I *had to* move on to the next work order. Other techs had been picking up the slack since I took on the Lister job, but it was time for me to return to earth. The man hadn't even called to inquire about his order. And no, I was not permitted to contact him. Not ever.

Ignoring her directive, I found Obediah's information on the order form, and tried calling his home from my cell. Met with the voice of a young girl, I quickly pressed "End."

—

The "News of the Weird" showed an old picture of Obediah from, I would guess, the 1990s—the last gasp of the analog camera. Underneath it, the caption, "Texas Man Dies Writing Prophecy . . . in Blood."[1]

Obediah had lost his mind and broke into a branch library in Houston after-hours. There was a quote from a lady who works the circulation desk, saying he had been a frequent visitor there, and would use their public computers every day, sometimes from 9 A.M. until closing

---

[1] As plugged-in readers are aware, this headline was hot on the shock-news circuit, and has led to an unfortunate meme, spawning virally into "Ack! Cathy Guisewite Dies Writing Comic Strip 'Cathy'... in Blood," "Fortune Cookie Writer Dies Writing His Own Fortune... in Blood," and "Internet Comedy Writer Dies Writing Internet Comedy... in Bloo—Agh!", each repetition revealing our deep discomfort in the presence of the inexplicable.

hour. But on this occasion, finding the computers shut down and the building closed, and suddenly convinced that his whole body had transformed into a quill and inkstand, Obediah opened up each of his fingers one by one and wrote on the austere concrete walls of the library until he ran out of fluid.

By contacting the photographer listed in the article, I was able to acquire stills from the scene of "the accident" and, through digitally enhancing, view their contents. As it turned out, the words Obediah had written on the bare walls of the library were not a prophecy at all, but an epilogue to the *Textbook of Alternate History* that, because it moldered on my desk in the shop, he could not complete.

Sickened to learn that my greatest discovery—of multidimensional realities, simultaneously lived yet revealed to me alone—could be just the mad ramblings of an unbelievably prolific fictional historian, armed with mimicry and imagination, I remained in bed for days, despairing. So strange to think, those nights that I spent scrolling through that digital textbook, orbiting the farther atmosphere of logic, reveling in a renewed faith in the supernatural, that its mortal author had been wandering hungry through the streets of Houston, with no computer, and no blank surface to write upon, so that all he could do in the end was expunge his body's own ink.

In reading his work, had I been the one to kill him? Had I not waited a week to start reconstructing the drive, would he still be peacefully typing it at this moment? If, once started, I recognized in its contents a troubled mind in need of help, could I have orchestrated some kind of intervention? What if I had pursued it further, and went in search of him, and saved him, rather than just calling the phone number he'd given then pressing "End"? What if?

—

The last time I set foot in The Workshop, I walked into the storefront because I was no longer employed as a tech. I showed the Textbook to Linda, insisting that we had a moral obligation to Mr. Obie Lister: to honor his strange legacy, to make real the alternate world that he had willed into existence. She looked at me with managerial concern.

She had checked the hard drive, and found it unworkable; she had checked my backups, and found them blank; she had checked the public record, and found no trace of Obediah Lister other than the "News of the Weird" and the work order. All she had left was a couple hundred handwritten pages hastily scrawled in the dark, and my word as to their origin.

Now it is too late, and I am left with a thousand questions about Obediah Lister and his thousand lost books. But the past is, as ever, the past, and history is, forever, history, and we cannot go back and cry out "Do over! Do over!" the way we used to, and relive the same story over again. When we try, we encounter the landscape of Guilt. And that is a terrain I refuse to wander. For, as the dead man speaking in his dead language said, through echoes of the printed word: HIC SVNT LEONES. Lions dwell here.

The Great Pyre of Egypt

A RUINED BOAT, A MINOR PYRAMID, a crucible once used as a pyre, and an amulet recovered from the remains of a vulture were all discovered engraved with the name and title of Khufu, each with a different year of kingdom certifying his death, which suggested to Egyptologists that either several Pharaohs ruled under the same name, or the Pharaoh had many impostors throughout the land.

The mystery of Khufu—of why he was buried so many times and in so many ways—was finally put to rest in

1954, when archaeologists discovered this papyrus scroll among papers used to line the sarcophagus of Khufu's grandson, Cheops III. It explains how Khufu exhaustively tested the burial rituals of all the religious cults.

The following text was written by Menefre, scribe to Cheops II, fourth Pharaoh of the XII Dynasty, who recorded the oral histories of the two preceding kings, whom he served as a former slave of the Pharaoh's court.

—

The hennu boat sailed slowly on to dusk, carrying the body of Khufu downstream. The mourners knelt in the Nile's reedy banks. A copper horn sounded thrice: once for the lower kingdom, once for the upper kingdom, and once for the Pharaoh who united them. There was no wind to carry the sound, so that the intonations hung in the air like vapor.

The concubines were most convincing in their wails of grief; they had devoted their lives to pleasing the Pharaoh. The priests and courtiers who had been forced to attend stared out upon the scene stoically; the peasants who had come down to the river that evening to retrieve their nets looked bewildered by the ceremony.

The silent ripples of wood on water trailed behind him. Finally, Khufu sat up in the boat, shaking off the scepter and Book of the Dead, and uncrossing his arms from his chest. "This won't do," he said, scanning the surface of the river for signs of disruption. The waters hardly moved at all. "At least we could have chosen a day when the Nile was high, when the river moves faster than a cattle's pace. At this rate, my soul would reach paradise before my body ever reached the Delta."

The high priest of Seker called out, "Pharaoh, we are all ashamed. Seker must know your soul is not separating from your body, so halted the winds to rebuke you."

His third funeral had been the most disappointing. He could not help but feel that all the ceremony and ostentation was wasted on the dead. "This is pageantry," said the Pharaoh. "This is how they bury the dead in Memphis?" Khufu asked.

"Not *all* dead. The poor are put into the river. But those who can afford to, take the hennu boat down to the Delta."

The Pharaoh sighed a sigh of pity for the rich men of this land.

Under the light cascading from the atrium at the temple of the sun, the priests of Amon took turns appealing to Pharaoh's sense of history, loyalty, and grandeur. Each had their own notions as to how the Pharaoh should be honored after death. The crux of the discussion came down to this: should the Pharaoh, in death, strive toward *neheh*, the eternity of the Nile—flooding, receding, renewing with every season? Or should he embody *djet*, the eternity of the mountain: stony, fixed, and unchanging for centuries?

Horeb, a shipbuilder, was still of the opinion that the only way to truly recognize the Pharaoh's divinity over the land was to send him in a boat down the Nile River. Mishrata, a wagoneer, suggested that the Pharaoh should be taken out into the desert and placed face-up in the sun, positioned so that his body would be stretched to its limit, until the vultures accept him, piece by piece, into their bodies. A vulture-headed god was proposed for just this purpose. And an architect, Imenhotep, suggested a grand mausoleum with four sides that tapered to a point, built so sturdily that it would not fade for five thousand years.

In the months to follow, each would be put to the test, and each would achieve nothing but the Pharaoh's disappointment. He wanted a death undeniably holy, and not mere spectacle. The gathering ended moodily, with the Pharaoh retiring to his own corner, brooding on the poverty of vision among his courtiers. Whatever else happened in his life, and in his reign over Egypt, Khufu swore, his manner of death must be perfect.

In his chambers, Khufu reclined on his ivory headrest and sighed. World-weariness is a common lament of kings, but this breath exhaled from a deeper source. The concubine dancing on the floor in front of him continued what would otherwise have been tantalizing enticements. Nearby, Shamisé, who was older and more experienced, took the King's sad breath as an invitation.

"Khufu, what is your despair?" she said. "You will make Nafrit believe that she is not a skillful dancer."

Khufu cast a dark eye toward Shamisé, then closed his

29

eyes and lay back, concentrating on the patterns of light on the insides of his lids.

"Ignoring it is not enough. Tell Shamisé what is troubling you," she said, leaning over to stroke the forehead of the Pharaoh. She dabbed oil on his temples, and let it drip down to his neck before rubbing it into his skin. He aimed a confiding stare at his first and most beautiful concubine.

"Nothing I have ever done will be remembered. They do not raise statues to your name for keeping peace."

Shamisé laughed an echoing laugh, and the Pharaoh's brow darkened with twin lines pointing outward from the center, like footprints in the sand. "If the Pharaoh wants statues," she said, "the Pharaoh can build statues. It doesn't take an army to sculpt your face in stone."

"It's something else . . ." Khufu continued to stare into Shamisé. "I don't *want* to be remembered. I fear . . ." He could not think of the word "judgement."

"Does the Pharaoh speak of fear? Even gods tremble at your name. The armies of every kingdom recede before you and their monarchs bow at your feet . . ." Shamisé said, prepared to continue until the Pharaoh's dark mood lifted, but he cast a stern eye on her and shook his head.

"Do not placate me," he said. Shamisé moved in close and pressed her cheek against his, catlike. "I fear the permanence of death, but even moreso do I fear the permanence of what I leave behind."

Shamisé pulled away, and frowned back at Pharaoh. "Shame on you. You are given divine status by birthright, and you speak to a concubine about the burdens of immortality." Then, a moment too late, Shamisé put on a smile to show that her rebuke was in jest.

Khufu put his hands on Shamisé's hips, leaning her against the wood frame of the bed and raising his body above hers on the rush mat. Her teasing smile excited him, and he suddenly desired to claim her. But persistent thoughts of death had drawn the blood away from his sex, and in the end he had to clench himself to sleep.

Imenhotep, Pharaoh's architect, advocated a burial both traditional and revolutionary. In Saqqara, stone pyramids were erected which showed the vastness of the Pharaoh's power and his closeness to the gods. But Imenhotep's own design was greater than all those that had come before it.

Starting with a one-quarter scale step pyramid, Giza's laborers, all of whom had been conscripted to serve the Pharaoh's command, worked for seven months to construct the site of what could have been Pharaoh's final resting place. The workers themselves—masons, potters, weavers, carpenters—interrupted their lives and livelihoods to build the Pharaoh's tomb, and the vizier who commissioned them was reluctant to let them know that the great structure to which they leant their expertise was only the stage for a drama *enacting* the Pharaoh's funeral, his fourth this year.

Imenhotep dispensed with tunnels, and had them build a great room, which was decorated exactly the same as the Pharaoh's private room. This included the beds and decorations and smallest details of his living quarters. This was the Pharaoh's *diwan*, his home in death.

They began to wrap the King. The wet papyrus clung to his body like sinuous leeches. In just under an hour, the pith would be dry, and the Pharaoh unable to move in his sarcophagus.

The porous sheets had already begun to stiffen when he was lowered into the gold-inlaid coffin. He breathed intensely through the airhole as his sight fell under a slab of darkness. This time it began to feel real. He could imagine eternity. He could apprehend, finally, the ubiquity of death, the awful stillness of it, the self and all its notions of immortality become yet another soulless object. The sensation of nothingness, that ineffable sinking knowledge of consciousness as but a brief span of light between two eternal darknesses; it was the most harrowing thing the Pharaoh had ever known. Yet he clung to it for a long moment, as though it were an amulet warding off evil. Then, at that crescent edge of time where the length of a moment blurs, he called out, "Release me! Release me from this bondage!"

When the sarcophagus was opened, and the mummified Pharaoh cut out, water was poured on him to spill away the last crust of powder still clinging to his skin, leaving starchy patches where sweat had pooled.

"What a terrible way to honor death!" Khufu declared. "*This* is how they treat the men and women of Saqqara?"

"Only nobles of highest birth may have themselves buried in this fashion," explained Imenhotep who, upon having his creation thus spurned, could not conceal a scornful glance in the direction of this ungracious god. "The poor are thrown into the desert to wither in the sun."

"Even burning a man would be more honorable than wrapping him in paper and shutting him up in a tomb," Khufu growled, standing up and holding out his arms to be cleaned, which I coated with cypress oil and ash.

At this, Rami the merchant stepped forward and knelt before Pharaoh. "Great Pharaoh: as a merchant, I have travelled beyond the borders of Egypt, past Phoenicia, and seen many cultic rites and funereal practices. Nowhere have I seen a people so in awe of the majesty and power of death as in the mountains of the East, where the dead are turned to ashes by means of a funeral pyre. There are great gatherings of people, solemnly united in harmonious purpose, in thrall to the god that wrought such a spectacle."

Pharaoh pondered this for a moment, but staring

forward all the while, as though incapable of doubt. "We will explore this further. But how can we stage a burning?"

"Alcohol, which burns clean, allows liquid to ignite on the surface of the skin, without charring the flesh. This, too, I have witnessed," said the merchant Rami.

Pharaoh waited. His advisors were silent, uncertain whether these dry runs for death would continue indefinitely, or whether this burial would be his last—or, conceding Pharaoh's mortality, his next-to-last.

"It will be my next funeral," Pharaoh declared, and a collective sigh of relief was released from the noblemen.

Back in the Pharaoh's palace, I, then a Nubian slave, bathed Khufu's feet in salts and rubbed them with oil. Shamisé stood a few steps back, in the arched doorway of his chambers, waiting for the Pharaoh to be made clean.

"Nothing I do is sufficient," Khufu said, unable, it seemed, to turn his mind to the sight of his first and most beautiful concubine, or to the warm sensation in his toes. "I am not a conqueror. But I am a conqueror's son. And I am not the voice of god, as I am said to be."

Shamisé waved me away, and took over the duty of rubbing the oil into the Pharaoh's feet and legs. "You're right," said Shamisé. "You are not the voice of god. You *are* a god."

Somehow, this truth failed to fill Khufu with a sense of godliness, as was intended. Instead, he was distracted by the hands of his concubine, which spread the oil further along his sides. Whatever coils of nerve there were set themselves to flame, and the hot balm in her hands lifted his sleeping sex from its resting place, like a snake charmer. Feeling at last the stirrings of the Apis bull, excited by the scent of Hathor, the goddess of cows, embodied in the woman Shamisé, Khufu seized upon his passion and thrust her down into the cypress oil, falling upon her and letting it seep into them both, until they slithered back to his chambers, and the bed, where after he conquered his concubine, sleep found him.

From his height on the dune, with down-drifting gusts that conspired with the sun to tease the skin, Pharaoh looked at the thin Egyptians gathered below like vertical lines on the sand, shadowless. The attendance for each ceremony grew in number from the last, so that this, his fifth funeral, was visited by men and women from Upper Nubia, my old countrymen, a desert people who had for several months heard tales of the god-king who died and was reborn.

The plan was simple: the Pharaoh is doused with alcohol and set afire. Once he raises his right arm, suggesting that he has had enough of this death—that he knows how such a ceremony would feel, look, smell, and sound—sand is poured over him, smoldering the flame and cooling him off until his senses return.

The day was perfect for burning. It was noon, and the white-hot desert sun was at its zenith. Pharaoh stood in the man-sized crucible—a great bowl from which a titan might have taken his meal—arms out at his sides, and the pure alcohol poured in a delicate coat over his skin, collecting in the crucible, mixing with sand. The Pharaoh of all Egypt, god-king and emperor, stood naked and wet in the warming sun.

As the high priest of Amon, god of the sun, lit the fire at Pharaoh's feet, which burned blue, many craftsmen in the desert that day thought of the kilns in which they fired *faience*, the pottery paste that hardens into a glossy, supernatural blue. Fulfilling this image was the Pharaoh himself, who wore the *Khepresh*, the blue crown of war. And there was something statuesque about the figure of the Pharaoh, poised with his arms wide and his knees slightly bent, like a falcon for flight, utterly nude but for the one regalia. The flames engulfed him. Two slaves stood by with sacks full of sand, to pour over the Pharaoh at his signal. His arms remained level with his shoulders.

It was Shamisé who first saw the skin of the Pharaoh rupturing, blackening, or, at least, was the first to shout, "The oil! The oil! Pharaoh is burning!"

Yet no one could react. Pharaoh's arms remained still. No one dared oppose his sacred commands. We waited, and waited, for his signal; until his torso and limbs collapsed into the bowl at his feet, then slowly incinerated into nothing, and by the time it was near-dark and we were forced by an approaching storm to seek shelter, it dusked upon us that *this* must be the way that Pharaoh had wanted it all to end.

—

According to Menefre, who recorded this as Amon's first miracle, Khufu's remains were utterly incinerated, leaving nothing but ash, mixed with dust, out of which protruded fragments of sharp, shining crystal. Historians who credit Menefre's account surmise that the intensity of heat from the sun, together with the oil-burning fire, using his body as its kindling, was enough to incinerate his bones, and to transmute the sand at his feet to glass, which shattered when his bones collapsed.

Though it made a spectacle in his time, Khufu left nothing behind for posterity except one temple from his reign, and some records—lists, mostly, of days and years, and items from his treasury, and the names of his one hundred concubines, with the ideogram for Shamisé shown face-forward: a picture unlike any hieroglyph until the reign of Nefertiti.

CHAPTER 1:

The Great Pyre of Egypt

Suggestions for Class Discussion:

Did Khufu intend for his last funeral ceremony to be a suicide? Was it due to his shame as a conqueror? Why did he decline to construct the tomb designed by Imenhotep, which would have writ his legacy on the very land of Egypt for thousands of years, electing instead to be burnt to nothing? What would Egypt look like today had the Pharaohs been buried in stone, rather than reduced to ashes and cast to the wind?

CHAPTER 2

Siddhartha Remains in His Father's Palace

SIDDHARTHA GAUTAMA, "Emperor of Kapilavastu" (c. 563–483 BCE), is known as the ancient world's most successful conqueror, whose empire spans two continents and encompasses millions of citizens, soldiers, and slaves. Yet accounts from his early life suggest that Siddhartha was once tempted by a different destiny.

Ananda, cousin to Siddhartha, gave this account of the

strange circumstances of his birth: "Before Prince Siddhartha Gautama was born, Queen Mahamaya dreamt of giving birth to a white elephant. From this auspicious dream, the one hundred astrologers prophesied that her son would become either a great conquerer, or a holy man. But the Queen Mahayama died during the birth of her son, before she could know anything of his fate.

"Suddhodana, the king, hated the thought of his son as an ascetic—self-denying and content with nothingness—a pretender to godliness. So Suddhodana shuttered away his son in a palace as large as a city, away from the sight of human suffering, and gave him every comfort, as long as he vowed never to venture beyond the palace walls."

Our selection, excerpted below, was written by Channa, Siddartha's groom, charged with protecting the Prince's innocence.

It is called the Guardian's Scroll, as it records Channa's efforts to protect Prince Siddhartha from the influences of moral and intellectual corruption.

—

In our home, instead of tears, we had proverbs. Instead of windows, we had murals high as the ceiling and wide as the walls. The great hall was filled with statuary, engraved columns, and bas-reliefs depicting Sakyamuni's history, each war, each triumph and tragedy in its remote, ancestral glory. In the stories of the ancients, say the court poets, the innocent and proud-hearted prevail over the corrupt.

The palaces in our stone archipelago were lit by a courtyard through which we could see the walls of the palace that stood directly across (one palace for each season of the year). But there were no openings at all that faced outward, toward the world.

Above the Autumn Palace could be seen the head of a tall banyan tree. It was the farthest object the Prince's eyes had ever witnessed. The banyan tree became the symbol for all of life's limitations: he could conceive of nothing farther, larger, or more ancient than the old banyan tree. For the Prince and the world had never been introduced.

Instead, the world was brought to him—object by object, pleasure by pleasure. A wreath of jewels, a sculpture of ice, exotic musical instruments and exotic performers to play them. Everywhere were refinements of the soul, fine food and tasteful art, the best of everything made by man—all of it purchased by his oath of isolation—and the best of everything made by god: the beauty of women in the bud of youth; high-flying acrobats and gymnasts performing unnatural feats of flexibility and strength; conjurers weaving impossible illusions; animal curiosities and rare orchids from distant jungles.

The most formidable challenges I faced, as guardian of Siddhartha Gautama, the Sakyamuni, were the most common human acts—the ebb and flow of everyday feeling that threatened at any moment to burst forth like a cracking dam. The longer we deferred the grieving of that child—motherless, free of any suffering that might cause him to compare his present state of contentment with the dawning realization of the world's temporality—the more I feared its inevitability.

But that tidal wave never came. *And every dawn the dying rose was plucked, the dead leaves hid, all evil sights removed: For said the King,* "If he shall pass his youth far from such things as move to wistfulness and brooding on the empty eggs of thought, the shadow of his fate, too vast for man, may fade, and I shall see him grow to that great stature of fair sovereignty, when he shall rule all lands—if he will rule—The king of kings and glory of his time."[2]

In my care, under his father's roofs, the Prince would indeed become the king of kings and glory of his time, and need never brood on the empty eggs of thought.

Siddhartha's library was vast and varied, and he had read nearly everything in it. By his eighteenth year, he knew every word of wisdom uttered by every wise man the world had known. Whenever his cousin Ananda came to him with some dilemma or mystery, Siddhartha would always have an answer, but recited it impassively, as though it were merely life's instructions, evident to anyone with enough clerical acumen to find them.

Since Siddhartha spent so much time cloistered in the library, I too spent my days among the rough hide covers and the oversized scrolls upon which the ancient words were written—the frail and dusty textures of the Prince's youth. But on the rare occasion when I would cross the

---

[2] Steel, Henry. *The Life of Buddha and Its Lessons.*

threshhold into the world at large, leaving Siddhartha behind, I often returned to find him wandering among the books, pale and hungry from neglect. My other duty was to remind the Prince of his obligations to the body.

I lacked the discipline to know the texts intimately, so I begged Siddhartha to tell me the histories found there. In exchange, Siddhartha asked me to tell him stories of the wider world. Against my better judgment, I indulged the Prince. The most mundane detail could ignite the deepest rapture within the Prince's heart, coming as it did with the authority of experience, that it was an event to which I had borne witness, and not a relic of the ancients.

But if I anticipated danger in these exchanges, it proved unfounded. It was not possible for Siddhartha to see any connection between the stories in books, and those I told to him about the world. For him, the whole world seemed to exist within the walls of the Four Palaces. And the whole of life seemed to exist in the span between his ears.

There had been moments before in his life when I felt my duty as protector of His Majesty's innocence was in jeopardy. The first was when Siddhartha was introduced to his teacher, Visvamitra, who, seeing the boy's innate powers of mind, bowed before the child all the way to the floor, as though he were a god. There was a spark of recognition in the eyes of the Prince, so swift that it passed without notice among all in our company. But, in that moment between the teacher prostrating himself before the Prince as he would a holy man, and his removal, Siddhartha must have secretly glimpsed his other destiny.

Then there was the Prince's first meeting with Yasodhara, his betrothed, in the circular garden, surrounded by bellflowers. Until this encounter, all the women the Prince had known existed merely for his amusement, but Yasodhara, rather than teasing and titillating the Prince, conversed with him, asking who was responsible for the care of his precious gardens. "I am," the Prince replied, for he had no way of knowing that each night the garden was tended for him by his servants.

Yasodhara, the King admitted, was unpredictable; her sly instinct for rebellion had been noted, but after all, she herself had had the most sheltered youth of all of

Siddhartha's prospective wives, the most like his own. Yasodhara's father joked with Suddodhana that he feared his daughter might be *too* innocent, and unsure of what to do in the marriage bed. But in the end the business of women and men took care of itself.

At the age of twenty-nine, Siddhartha became a father. His first wife Yasodhara gave birth to a healthy, flawless boy. No auspicious dreams were recorded. No astrologers were summoned to prophesy his future. And the baby did not stand up and speak as Siddhartha himself was said to have done upon his birth. But when Siddhartha offered to his infant son his hand, the boy seized one finger with unusual force and held it in front of him with both hands. His grip was so powerful that it closed over the finger and locked like a shackle, and so Siddhartha named the boy *Rahula*, or "fetter."

When Rahula was but a few days old, he opened his eyes and fixed them on his father's face. The two princes stared long and long, absorbed in each other's mutual innocence. The visage of the elder prince—usually

deadened with some new pleasure or momentary fancy—
was *alive* with pain.

I do not know what Siddartha felt at that moment. The
Prince kept his counsel. But I know what any man must
feel when he beholds the fruit of his loin, marking the
distance between his unremembered origins and his aging
body. It requires no special insight or education to feel
life's quickening, and to apprehend, physically, its import.

But whereas Siddhartha's birth had filled his father with
a fierce resolve to mold him into a man of untold greatness,
the revelation brought on by his own son took the form of
an uncertainty which would not be reconciled until death.

The greatest threat to our Prince's purity was a simple
chariot ride through the Prince's pleasure park, not long
before the events recounted here. By the will of the gods,
an elderly man had found his way inside the palace walls to
the park, and looked meaningfully toward us as we trotted
in his direction. There were grooves in his forehead and
cheeks like rivers cutting gorges into dry land; eyes that
were heavy-lidded on top *and* bottom, so that you could

see the full shape of each globe encased within its wrapping; a grizzled brown-gray beard with spots of deep shadow like currants in a bowl of porridge. "What is the matter with that man?" Siddhartha asked, pointing at the old man, innocent of modesty. "Has he been burned, or was he born that way?"

Knowing that the Prince intended to spend the afternoon in the pleasure park, but observing how the gods sought to interfere with my sacred duty, I was struck mute with indecision. But in protecting the Prince's innocence, I have learned that hesitation in a lie is worse even than steadfastness in the truth. If you reveal any uncertainty, man's curiosity will prevail.

I answered, "It is a problem afflicting that man only. It is a family curse, and has nothing to do with Your Majesty or his kin." Then I reined in the mighty horse Kanthaka and turned it around, heading into the palace where there was no old age, sickness, or death.

A hand on my shoulder shook me awake. I looked up from midst a dream of some strange war. In this dream, beasts were turned to children, children were turned to soldiers, and soldiers were turned to demons. For a moment I dwelled in half-dream, shrinking from the approach of a many-toothed demon, until I recognized the voice of Prince Siddhartha. "Channa, I am leaving the palace. I have lived for too long in a decorous prison, and I am thirsty to drink from a fountain that does not flow from Suddodhana's streams. I must fly. And you must help me. Fetch Kanthaka, and wait for me at the gate."

"But, Your Majesty, the gate is too heavy for even a hundred men to lift." I appealed to him humbly, with my hands folded and head bowed.

"We can leap over it. In all the land, a better steed has never stamped the earth." Siddhartha made for the door, and I stepped in his way.

"Your Majesty, there are a thousand guardsmen outside the palace walls, all of whom are sworn to keep us. And beyond the one thousand guardsmen, there are one thousand foot soldiers, and beyond the one thousand foot soldiers, one thousand cavalrymen."

"When they see my determination," said the Prince,

"they will part like a river at a crossing."

My eyes darted around in the darkness, fixing on nothing but shallower depths of the selfsame darkness. "And the King?" I asked.

To this, there was a hair's width of hesitation. "He was wrong," said the Prince, as if the King were but another hurdle in his path. "The future cannot be prophesied."

Donning robe and sandals, I lit a lamp. I could hardly focus, but for the fact that I'd spent my life in fear of this moment and was roused by the thought of my execution.

In the lamplight I continued to search the room for an explanation. "But, Master, why?"

To this inquiry the Prince had already devised an answer. "Because I left my mother's womb, though it killed her. But I have never left my father's womb."

But if it does not kill your father, I ached to say, *he will surely kill* me. Yet I knew of only one set of hands strong enough to hold the Prince's reins. "Yes, Your Majesty. The Sakyamuni is righteous, his decrees are just, and wisdom is his birthright. But do this: *go to Rahula*. Bid farewell to your son, as he will be but an orphan to your memory."

The Prince wore a smile that was not a smile.

I followed the Prince into his chambers. There lay Rahula, more peaceful than a sage, untroubled by any knowledge that makes one restless in sleep.

Dawn gathered through the windows. In the reddening light, Siddhartha appeared as a sillhouette, a blur, like a double image, a man cleaved in two by the sun's rays. Half of him reached toward the child and lifted him into his arms; half of him shut his eyes and turned his chin away.

The illusion persisted long enough to convince my senses of its absolute veracity, until the Prince finally coalesced and appeared as he would in the natural world, holding the infant son as he awoke to the morning sounds.

Those wakeful eyes! Those world-absorbing eyes! The infant's stare had an animal fascination that rendered the Prince's quest for the self (or the loss of self) irrelevant; what soul was to be found, could be found here; what immortality was to be found, could be found here; what knowledge, what wisdom, what mindfulness . . .

"I am your student," the elder prince said to his son, his eyes becoming loose and liquid in a way that came upon

Phong Nguyen

him unbidden and unforeseen.The child had rendered him into stone, as I had predicted. I thanked the gods, knowing that Siddhartha would not leave the palace as planned. That he would never abandon the world that he knew.

Then came Suddodhana, the king with silent mouth and deafening eyes. Siddhartha turned away and felt still his father's gaze, as though it were the heat of the sun: a light that skin can feel. He stood in his night garment, a scant wrap that only served as a reminder that the King stood in the arched doorway without his clothes. His face was line-worn from the uneasy sleep of kings, and his body showed all the texture of age. Yet still he projected royalty.

The King was no orator. He began every address to the people by saying, "Speeches are the refuge of men who have failed in action." But in this moment the King's silence was greater than the absence of sound—it flowed outward, encompassing the Prince Siddartha, and the young Prince Rahula, who bathed in the warm light of dawn, reflecting it from his infant skin like the curve of the new moon. And when the father spoke, it was without its usual commanding tone.

"*Now*," he said, "you know," and his very voice seemed to hold each of them aloft like a jeweller lifting precious stones one by one to the torchlight.

—

Because of Channa's guardianship, Siddhartha would become the ruler that he was ever destined to become.

Though Channa ceased to be active in the court soon after Siddhartha assumed the mantle of King of Sakyas, then Emperor of Kapilavastu and its vast colonies, it was by his influence that the fate of the young Prince did not stray from his father's path. Few scholars have recognized what careful stewardship it took to protect the Prince from the merest hint of sickness, old age, and death. But if the Prince's father was its commissioner, then Channa was its executor. Just as the boy Siddhartha grew up learning the great war stories of his forebears, his own victories would, in turn, become a thing of legend, his conquests immortal; his martial legacy unsurpassed in the annals of history.

CHAPTER 2:

Siddhartha Remains in His
Father's Palace

Suggestions for Class Discussion:

Knowing his infamous bloodlust on the battlefield, could
Emperor Siddartha actually have become a sage, as the one
hundred astrologers predicted? Why was it necessary to
keep the Prince away from any evidence of human frailty?
How might this have led to a misfire of fate? What does
King Suddodhana's experiment in mental and bodily
indulgence say about the soul of man?

CHAPTER 3

Plato, King of Syracuse

WHEN DIONYSUS II FIRST OFFERED to Plato the city of
Syracuse, jewel of Sicily, for the philosopher to rule as his
own, there was a pall of doubt. The last time Plato had
come to Sicily, he was thrown in prison and sold into
slavery. But this time, after dialoguing with his students,
and a sober visit to the temple of Athena, he accepted the
burden of leaving his beloved Akademeia to make the
utopia of his famed *Republic* a living reality.

Though Plato was given Syracuse to rule as his own,

Dionysus II remained emperor of Sicily, levying onerous taxes on the city, which the utopia could not support.

Demosthenes, an orator and former student of Plato's, wrote this account of Plato's first days as ruler of Syracuse, in his series on kings. The portrayal of Plato offered here suggests that the king of Syracuse was a greater philosopher than he was a ruler of men.

—

At the first meeting of the Nocturnal Council, there was barely any light from the Mediterranean dawn, and all the philosopher kings stood leaning on their canes and looking weary. But farm-born Theocritus, poet of Syracuse, stood amongst them, eyes peeled wide, exposing his shepherd thinness and obsidian skin from years of toiling in the Sicilian sun—as Theocritus was once a laborer, and the only native of Syracuse among them.

"Guardians of Syracuse," he said, speaking loudly to compensate for the gestures that were lost to the near-dark. "I do not bring my troubles here to burden you with private affairs, but to show respect for the new state. It is loyalty to Syracuse—no matter who rules her—that guides me."

At this moment, Plato's eyes wandered—not to suggest a waning of his attention, but to gauge the reaction of the councillors. Eloquence in oratory being yet another reason to root out the sophistic influence of the false poet.

"Yesterday, Xenocrates came to my home, as a representative of this Council, and sat with me and my sons. After drinking of the milk from my cattle, and eating of the fruits from my orchard, this noble guardian informed me that I was to cease hereafter the writing of poetry. In one breath, Xenocrates meant to erase my livelihood and my legacy. What was his reason for demanding such a revolution in my affairs? For the good of the children of Syracuse!"

Theocritus then turned to face Xenocrates directly, whom he identified even in the dimness. "I have raised four sons into men—*men* of Syracuse who have fought in two of our wars, and one of whom died for the honor of Greece. I know what I have suffered on behalf of the children of Syracuse. What of you, Xenocrates?"

Plato then stepped forward and took Theocritus in hand, as if the proceedings of the court were merely a conversation between the two—a teacher and his student, walking among the pillars of the Parthenon in a distant Akkadian city.

"Theocritus, all that we decide, we decide for the good of Syracuse. We do not impose laws at the expense of freedom, but we mean to persuade you of the rightness of acting according to these laws. Would you agree that a just society is a society that voluntarily adheres to its laws?"

"I would."

"So then it would follow that the crucial point in this matter is not whether you can be compelled to act according to our wishes, but whether we can persuade you of our view regarding the writing of poetry."

"I would say so, yes, but it will be exceedingly difficult to change my mind concerning the virtues of poetry."

"I am glad that you are quick to speak of virtue, Theocritus. I am especially keen to know whether you believe that poetry can inspire us toward the virtues of courage, wisdom, moderation, and justice."

"I do believe it," said Theocritus.

"Would you agree that poetry can also inspire us toward the corruption of virtue—cowardliness, idiocy, excess, and injustice?"

"I cannot think of an instance where it has, but I would say that it is possible."

Plato smiled generously at the younger man. "So if good poetry instructs us in the virtues, and bad poetry instructs us in the corruption of virtues, would you agree that poetry has the potential for both positive and negative influence?"

Theocritus' eyes lit up. "But this is precisely my point, Plato. That poetry can be used constructively or destructively, like anything else. We cannot forbid the use of the chisel just because it can also be used for harm."

"But, Theocritus, in the case of poetry, it is possible to separate the good uses from the bad. Would you be opposed even to the censorship of bad poetry?"

"I would," said Theocritus.

"Are you so fond of bad poetry that you wish to promote it, though it distracts from the good?"

"I am not so fond of bad poetry, as you say, but it is necessary that a poet remain free to write poorly so that he may write well."

"It seems to me that this is a sophistic statement," said Plato, who by his tone appeared to sense how the two men were speaking perpendicularly to each other.

"Even so," said Theocritus, narrowing his eyes to communicate his resolve.

Plato looked up to see the sun crowning over a line of trees in the distance. "Will you agree to meet again, you and I, to decide what is an appropriate degree of self-censorship in the writing of poetry?"

Theocritus furrowed his brow, and moved his eyes from Plato to the Council and back again. He had come to the Council expecting a fight, or worse, a trial and execution, as Dionysus would have had it. The heat in his chest and his hands bespoke a readiness for action. His body was disappointed by the aspect of peace it wore now.

So, the matter having been settled for the moment, and the sun rising swiftly above Sicily, the Nocturnal Council dispersed and Theocritus returned home.

——

Plato stood straight and parallel to the cane in his left hand. The vanity of a knobby wooden cane was one of the few indulgences he permitted himself as an old man. The fallow land below was spotted with stations where young Syracusans practiced their gymnastics, looking from this vantage like figures in an Oriental tapestry.

There were so many pleasures to be had from the looking, Plato thought. In another life, he might have been content to observe, but his circumstance demanded that he put into practice the principles that he formulated long ago. He walked down the path to the sandy field, accompanied by Adeimantus and Xenocrates, and all the youths gathered immediately around.

If there was one thing Plato disliked about the founding of a new Syracuse, it was the speech-making. Though oratory was taught in his Akademeia, and though his principles supported it, he found it to be personally distasteful. His penchant was, always, for dialogue. When it came down to it, he hated to espouse anything—he preferred the give and take of two honest souls in intellectual communion.

"Athletics are perfect," Plato reminded them. "Health cannot lead to illness, nor can illness come from health. It is impossible by definition."

"Reason is perfect," Plato said, "because it leads us to the true and the just . . ."

After Plato spoke, a skinny boy with lazy eyes approached, saying, "I am Dido, youngest son of Theocritus. I have heard the teachers say that, in our poesis, the writing of poetry should not be undertaken because of its falsity. My father is a poet by profession; is he a liar?"

Over the mossy stones they walked, overlooking the sandy beach. Plato invited Xenocrates to walk with him. "Shall this be our first act after the founding of the new Syracuse? Convincing children their fathers are dishonorable men?"

"It was made clear to me that the first priority of the ideal state is the education of children," said Xenocrates, evasively.

"And the education of men," said Plato, while the surf

crept closer to his sandals, and the wave sounds lulled them both into a quiet parlay.

"Yes," agreed Xenocrates. "And Theocritus' versifying is full of a falsity that corrupts the virtues, as you have established."

"Truly, Theocritus writes with indifference to the perfection of society, because we have not taught him to do otherwise. But you, Xenocrates," said Plato, who had the talent of tarnishing an idea without defiling its wearer, "have done Syracuse a greater disservice by using the authority of the Council to compel him to do so."

"I did as you asked, Plato, and endeavored to compel him to our view. But Theocritus—"

"Not compulsion," said Plato, "but education. We have perceived the truth ourselves through the rigorous pursuit of it. Now we must impart that truth to others. It is our duty. Anything but the pursuit of the good, in ourselves as well as in others, is unjust."

"I think you will find Theocritus immune to education," said Xenocrates, smiling.

"I have seen greater changes take place in this world

than one man's opinions," said Plato, accepting the terms of the implied challenge.

"Yes," said Xenocrates mistily. "This world is full of improbable things."

Plato and Theocritus sat alone among the ivy-covered stones. Occasionally Theocritus would stand up and pace back and forth on the gravel. Plato, at peace with his own doubts, remained seated with the cane on his lap.

"What about my bucolics? How can a pastoral poem about the love of a goatherd be said to lead to the loss of virtue?" Theocritus asked.

"It is not the goatherd's love that is corrupting, but the transformations of the gods in such a poem. The gods are perfect in their original forms, and any transformation is a diminishment. To suggest that the gods diminish themselves is false. The stories we tell to children are full of such metamorphoses, and this is precisely what perpetuates these myths. The young, who cannot distinguish between truth and falsehood, will learn to disrespect the gods, and to barter in lies."

Theocritus scowled, in spite of himself. "What of Homer? Is the poetry of Homer a lie?"

"The poetry of Homer is not only a lie," said Plato, "it is a bad lie."

"I do not see how I can converse with a man who is so hostile to poetry that he cannot see the good in Homer," Theocritus said, raising his voice in incredulity, while Plato remained steady and calm. "You, yourself—an Athenian!—grew into manhood reciting the poetry of Homer, yet you are able to find virtue in your own nature. How can that be, if the 'bad lies' of Homer have been corrupting you all these years?"

"Truly, it was through the education of Socrates."

"And Socrates? Didn't *he* grow up hearing and repeating the words of Homer?"

"I do not know by what divine wisdom Socrates lifted himself out of the cave of illusions and onto the firm ground of truth; nor how he came to return among us and impart that selfsame wisdom to the citizens of Athens. But I would not turn my back on his wisdom simply because he was once privy to the same epic lies as all Greeks."

"So how, then, do I compose poetry in a way that corresponds to your wishes?"

"By aspiring toward the good, and pointing the hearer toward the ideal."

"Why would I write only of the ideal, and ignore the reality around me? Isn't it your assertion that the aspiration of poetry should be truth? Which is it that you are against, Plato? Falseness, or reality?"

"Simulation of reality is falsity. Furthermore, it is sophism. Sophism is worse than plain ignorance or plain falsehood, because it pretends at truth and it persuades us of the false. Just so, poetry that pretends at reality, but comes only near enough to convince us that the illusion is the reality, is sophistic."

Theocritus paused, looking upward, as though the aegis of gods could shield him from logic. "I think I have an inkling of your meaning, Plato. When I hear a lesser poet imitate my work, the result is a mockery of the original. Even if the imitation is close to the mark—*especially* if it is close, without retaining the spirit of the former—the result is all the more offensive."

"And worse," said Plato, placing his hand affectionately at the knee of his charge, "the innocent listeners, when they finally come to hear the original, will be so tainted with the imitation that they will not know the difference."

Theocritus sighed, and shook his head. "I will try, dear Plato, for your sake, to write poetry that aspires to the good, that is not merely mimetic, but ideal. Even if it should mean an end to poetry."

"Yes," said Plato distractedly, his mind already turning toward the day's next task. "Reality is sufficient, and it does not need our embellishment."

"It will be difficult for me to turn my eyes from the reality I observe around me, Plato, and write only of ideal things, but I will try."

"And that is all that I ask," said Plato, patting the other on the shoulder, then using his cane to stand. "Now, I must cut short our disputation for the betterment of the state."

As Theocritus bade him farewell, and Plato took the first rise on the path in the slow way of a philosopher, he could not resist glancing smugly toward Xenocrates, who walked quietly beside him.

Meanwhile, as history records, Dionysus II had landed in Syracuse and sat awaiting Plato in the main palace. It was dark by the time Plato returned.

"And where were you off to this night, Plato, *King* of Syracuse?" asked Dionysus, enunciating *king* with all the subtlety of a blunt instrument.

"I am not a king. You gave me Syracuse to rule as I see fit, and I have instituted a guardianship consisting of thirty members. I am merely one of thirty."

"I am most eager to see how you control the population of the city. You will have a difficult time, I think, cutting Syracuse down to 5, 040 citizens."

"A perfect society such as we have imagined has never been seen before on earth. It will take considerable time, and even then, it will always remain at least one remove from the ideal," Plato reasoned.

"And was it the perfect society that kept me waiting for your return?" said Dionysus.

"That was Theocritus, the poet, whom I am instructing in the truth."

Dionysus' demeanor instantly changed. He lowered the

tip of his chin to the recess of his throat, staring up at Plato from under his perfectly trimmed eyebrows, triangles of shadow pointing downward from his sunken cheeks. That was his fearsomest quality—how suddenly his emotion shifted with the news. "When I made you King of Syracuse, the only condition I put upon you was that you take no other students but me! And not a month has passed before you take on another?"

"Theocritus is not a student, but a citizen. I am instructing him in the manner that a king instructs his subjects."

"But I *am* a king, and I instruct no one," Dionysus said.

Plato looked at him with a wan smile, as if to say he didn't doubt it.

Dionysus' face shifted again, and he extended an arm to the venerable Athenian. "Let us move to the agora to discuss our affairs, as they did in ancient times."

"Yes, let's," said Plato, his profound calm shaken by the volatile Emperor, whom he would always remember as an eleven-year-old child, full of arbitrary demands upon everyone within his voice's considerable range.

They strolled from the palace into the commons, to the agora where merchants and their slaves jostled one another and passersby for space. The Syracusans—who had been bowing at the feet of kings for centuries—knelt as the great men passed before them, though Plato knelt with them and reminded them again that Syracuse no longer had a king.

"I would have thought you could have done more by now," said Dionysus, after a while. When Dionysus spoke, he began at a whisper, so that the listener was bade lean toward him, but soon rose to an ear-piercing crescendo, as though before a crowd. "But it has been weeks and you have not proven anything but your own idleness. You spent the day conversing with a poet? Not even many poets, but a single poet? This while the rest of Sicily harvested—and what is more, made a gift to us of a portion of each harvest?"

"I did not accept your proposition to rule Syracuse merely because I wanted to test my philosophical assumptions, with respect, King Dionysus," said Plato, "but rather, because it follows my principles—that action and consequence must proceed from true ideas."

"You missed my meaning, Plato. For a great philosopher, you have a remarkable capacity to self-deceive." Dionysus looked away when he spoke, as though he were speaking not to Plato the man, but to Greece. "So that I am not mistaken again, allow me to educate *you*: if you do not tithe half of your earnings to us, then I will be forced to reconquer Syracuse in the name of Dionysus."

Plato stood dumb. His speechlessness was, for Dionysus, the reward for all his efforts.

"Perhaps if you weren't busy meddling with poets you would have already trained your warriors and launched conquests of your own," Dionysus said.

Plato looked at his hands, as if to find homilies written there, then up at Dionysus. "If a man is to be honored for his virtues, then his promises . . . must not be conditional," Plato reasoned, for the benefit of his former student.

But the look in Dionysus' eye repealed argument, confounded logic, and damned reason to futility. Like the cold, unblinking stare of a fish, it seemed to say, "Appetite is all."

Plato looked down, while the activity of the agora

bustled around him. There, he saw only a patch of dirt and his own sandaled feet. "So this is it? You offer me Syracuse to make into the Magnesia of my ideals, just so that you can prove my notions a failure by force? Did you give up Syracuse because you wished to conquer her twice?" And this, much to his own surprise—for Plato had been bred to war like every other Greek—brought the salt to his eyes. Among warriors, Spartans, among even the Persian hordes, Plato had encountered cruelty such as he believed unparalleled in the civilized world. Yet here, the joy with which the conqueror announced his next conquest brought new depth to his understanding of evil.

Oh, the philosopher reduced to tears! The boy-king standing revealed as a tyrant while his mentor sobs into the folds of his chiton! Would that there were a poet left in Syracuse to tell his tale!

—

Demosthenes, though a pupil of Plato's, and one of his strongest supporters, acknowledges that the philosopher's influence declined after the fall of Syracuse. Appeals to the public, to show how Syracuse was never given a real chance to flourish, fell on deaf ears. The Emperor Dionysus ensured that this would become yet another lesson on the limits of philosophy. Beyond Sicily, beyond Pelopennesia, the ancients ridiculed "empty theorizing" and "intellectualism," and applauded themselves, each and all, for remaining men of *action*.

CHAPTER 3:

Plato, King of Syracuse

Suggestions for Class Discussion:

If Plato's Syracuse hadn't been cut short by Dionysus of Sicily, could it have succeeded? What if Plato had not accepted the rule of Syracuse at all—would his notion of utopia have gained more traction with the people? Is there something Homeric in the whimsy of the gods, and the war that brought Syracuse to its knees?

CHAPTER 4

Jesus, Unforsaken

WHETHER JESUS CHRIST OF NAZARETH, a minor
prophet from the Hebrew Bible, was a living man or a
composite character from several narrative traditions has
long been the subject of theological speculation. The Book
of Jesus, following Malachi among the minor prophets, is
the primary subject of this speculation. Jewish exegesis
holds that Jesus was an Essene, an ascetic reformer who
opposed the exclusionary laws of the Pharisees. But an
apocryphal book of the New Judaic school, discovered

among the Dead Sea Scrolls, suggests that, rather than a reformer of Judaic thought, the prophet Jesus envisioned a revolutionary turn in Judaism that would have spawned a new religious tradition around the notion of his godhood.

From what has been set down in the Judas Scroll— written by the apostle Judas Iscariot—it is clear that Jesus' aspirations as a prophet exceeded his present place in the Jewish Bible. Excerpts from the Scroll, included below, show a Jesus ambitious to die on behalf of humanity, which he otherwise regarded as unreedemably sinful.

—

I had just popped the morsel of bread in my mouth when Jesus said it was his flesh. The pulpy mass on my tongue felt suddenly rubbery, and the aftertaste of wine took on a metallic savor, but I continued to chew out of politeness. The bread tasted fishy and thin, transubstantial. When Jesus invited us to his Seder, he said it would be his last meal before the coming crucifixion, but we had no inkling then that he had meant for us to be his cannibalizers.

After passing around the winegourd and the platter, Jesus stood up and said, "Take and eat; this is my body." The glances that stole around our company were like a weaver's needle, threading every face in the room like a stitch. Nervous sweat pooled on our necks. "And this is my blood of the covenant, which is poured out for the many forgiveness of sins. I tell you, I will not drink of the fruit of this vine from now on until that day when I drink it new with you in my Father's kingdom."[3]

What relief! Jesus was only speaking in metaphor. I allowed my jaw to resume its grinding of the bread. I'd known Jesus to renounce drink before, but this statement, with its premonition of death, was uncharacteristic in its morbidity. He seemed so certain of it; we almost believed, with him, that on this night he would be crucified.

I had just begun to recover from his announcement, and to partake of the other victuals, when Jesus spoke again. He said, to the twelve of us arrayed at his table, "I tell you, one of you will betray me."[4]

---

[3] Matthew 26:26–29.
[4] Matthew 26:21.

I looked around. As I surveyed the faces of Simon, James, Thomas, Thaddeus, Matthew, Simon who is called Peter, his brother Andrew, James and John (the sons of Zebedee), Philip, and Bartholomew, there were many flickering expressions of accusation, guilt, and puzzlement, sometimes passing from one to another in the same face within an instant. I had no mirror, but can only guess that my own countenance bespoke the confusion I felt. Murmurs of "Not me" and "Surely not I" passed from breath to breath. Our Rabbi's open-ended accusation left a hot fire of suspicion crackling in the middle of our party, and the smoke that arose from it choked our eloquence.

Instead of words, our mouths were all drawn into puckers, mouthing but not pronouncing, "Who?"

"The one who has dipped his hand into the bowl with me will betray me. The Son of Man will go just as it is written about him. But woe to that man who betrays the Son of Man! It would be better for him if he had not been born."[5] Jesus spoke with softness even as he condemned his betrayer.

---

[5] Matthew 26:23–4.

And I tried to remember, Was it *I* who dipped his hand into the bowl, or another? To which bowl was he referring? There *was* a woman with an alabaster bowl, before the supper, who had washed his feet in perfume made from pure nard, but she was not among our company now.

What does he mean? Tell me: is it *all* metaphor, Rabbi Jesus?

Our senses slowed and limbs drooping from the wine spirits, but the spirits within us still buoyant, we sang hymns until our voices grew hoarse, and our throats tickled from drink. We stumbled across Kidron Valley, to the Mount of Olives, where surely, we thought, the pure air and bracing cold would sober us. But even in the peaceful starlight of the olive grove, where Jesus had led us, the angels of paranoia were swarming about his head like a plague of insects.

He took Peter aside and put one arm around his shoulder confidentially, saying slurrily, "This very night, before the rooster crows, you will disown me three times."[6]

---

[6] Matthew 26:34.

Peter protested. "I never will. I would die first." Those gathered nearby echoed those same words in a repetitive chorus, so that the air was not clear of our protestations for several moments.

Jesus looked peeringly at his first apostle Peter, then turned away, toward the olive grove. The veiny and bulbous spears of the olive tree grew thickly from the trunks. Roots and rocks overlapped one another on the soil. The fruit of the tree itself ripened purple and testicular from every branch in spite of the cold.

Despite the tree's flowering, the spectral space that surrounded it appeared vaster, more encompassing than anything the desert could produce.

Feeling the mood darken, we moved on, guided by Jesus to the Garden of Gethsemane, our wobbling feet sore.

In Gethsemane, Jesus sank further into the abyss. Seeing him wander that night from darkness to darkness, then settle into that small garden under a new moon, was like watching a man resign himself to quicksand. He asked us to stay behind while he walked off to pray with Peter and the two sons of Zebedee. So we idled in a grassy place, a shady corner of the garden, and, numb with drink, I slunk in the direction of sleep. But in my last waking moments, I swear I saw the savior weeping into his cupped hands, head tilted back, as though drinking of his own tears.

When he returned red-eyed and found us all asleep, he shook us awake. "What are you sleeping for? Couldn't you keep watch for even an hour?" His eyes darted about, and his brow creased with disappointment; he seemed personally slighted at the thought of our sleeping while he remained awake. "Pray with me, so that we do not fall into temptation."[7]

He walked away to pray a second time, and, try as I might to stay awake and keep the vigil with Jesus, my body succumbed to the temptation of sleep.

Jesus woke me again, "Can't you stay awake? Why would you want to sleep on this night of all nights?" He went around shaking the other disciples, until we all sat propped up, bleary-eyed and red-cheeked.

---

[7] Matthew 26:40–1.

He repeated this pattern the night long, suffering from a frantic fear of being the last waking one.

The last time he woke me, he lifted me fully onto my feet. "Are you still sleeping? Look, it's almost morning, and I'm going to be arrested and crucified at any moment!"

I didn't know what to say. I wanted to console this unraveling god, but how can an apostle comfort his savior?

When the sun rose, as if on cue, a crowd came out from the valley, brandishing swords and clubs, calling out Jesus by name. I began to wonder if, after all, the prophecy was true, I would now have to watch Jesus crucified, and if one of us would be to blame. The thought was too horrific to bear: my doubt, his sacrifice, our friendship.

I embraced Jesus, throwing myself between him and the mob. But when I pulled back from our embrace, and looked upon Jesus' face, there was a stern look in his eyes. I realized, too late, that by trying to shelter him from the crowd, I had instead revealed him to it. "Do what you came for," he said to me, as though I had given him away—as though it were a betrayal.

"No, I . . ." I began to say, but my voice was drowned by the cries of the mob as they swarmed over us.

As they pulled Jesus away by the robe, one of our number leapt out, drawing his sword, and sliced off the ear of the high priest's servant. With his free arm, Jesus stayed the man's hand, saying, "Put your sword away, for all who live by the sword will die by the sword. I could call on the Lord and he would send twelve legions of angels to rescue me. But then how would the scriptures be fulfilled?"[8]

So this was what Jesus had been bracing himself for— fortitude in self-sacrifice, inhuman in its proportion, divine in nature. All the wandering, the vigils, the drink and the song, the raging in the darkness. It was a cleansing, a preparation for martyrdom. But the nobility of this act was lost on me; as his friend, I saw only the loss of him. No book could ever replace the man.

The high priest's men dragged Jesus behind like a slaughtered calf. He muttered to them as he was being led away, "Am I leading a rebellion, that you have come out with swords and clubs to capture me? Every day I sat in the

---

[8] Matthew 26:52–4.

temple courts teaching, and you did not arrest me . . ."[9] as his voice faded into the distance.

Every disciple went his own way, feigning indifference to the death of our Rabbi, lest we be seen as his accomplices. So on throughout the day I wondered, Was *I* Jesus' betrayer? Was he dying for *my* sins? The thought was so troubling to my conscience, if I thought it true I might have hanged myself from guilt.

The next time I saw Jesus it was at the Festival, and he was being paraded before the crowd, along with another Jesus, named Barabbas. His clothes had been dirtied and shredded, his body bruised and bloodied, but his spirit unbroken.

As was the custom on the day of Passover, Pilate stood before the crowd gathered there at the Festival, and made his pronouncement to free one of the two prisoners. "Which of the two prisoners shall I release to you?"[10] he asked.

---

[9] Matthew 26:55.
[10] Matthew 27:21.

The chief priests and the elders went around inciting the crowd to call for the release of Barabbas, but, in desperation, I called out from beneath my hood, before any other could, "Release Jesus Christ!" I repeated the chant, nudging those nearby to take up the chorus. A few did, but the clamor was interspersed with hisses and curses.

The two factions competed in the volume of their support. "Release Jesus Barabbas!" the priests shouted, seeking favor within the crowd. "Release Jesus Christ!" I and a smaller number of supporters shouted in return.

Pilate spoke again, saying, "This one is a murderer," pointing to Barabbas with his left hand, and then to Christ with his right: "and this one is a blasphemer, who claims to be the Messiah, the one true King of the Jews. So who shall I let go free?"

"Free Jesus!" they shouted in unison.

Pilate waved his arms until the din subsided. "Wait," said Pilate. "There are two Jesuses here: Christ and Barabbas. Which Jesus do you want?"

"Barabbas!" they shouted.

Pilate's eyes darted back and forth, surveying the crowd

uneasily. "Wait, wait . . ." he said. "Do you mean that you want Barabbas to be freed, or to be crucified?"

Seizing my chance, I cried, "Crucify him!" Knowing how difficult it can be to rescind an oath of execution, I meant to incite the crowd to violence. The blood of a murderer was now on my hands. I cried out for his death with whatever was left of me. And, to my endless gratitude, the crowd took up the cry, and took the lesser Jesus away to be tormented.

The centurions pushed the Rabbi Jesus from the crowd, where he suddenly appeared frail and mortal again. As I came near him smiling, he looked fiercely upon me, saying, "Judas, your betrayal today is far worse than yesterday. You have taken more than my life; you have stolen destiny from God."

If the Jesus of yesterday had been dreary, paranoid and edgy—today's Jesus was fearfully blank. He had suffered incommunicable torture and humiliation, and now there was no pain, only the tingling of the nerve to remind him of the presence of his body, which he could scarcely feel.

His vow at our last Seder—to swear off wine until his crucifixion day—was broken that very afternoon, when a merchant passed in front of us with bloated wineskins hanging off his handcart. In defense of the Rabbi, it was the heat of the day, and the wine was thick and sweet.

Walking among the dunes now, we wandered, as we once did, silently through the land of Israel.

We found ourselves entering Golgotha, the crucifixion grounds. How curious that our aimless stroll took us there. Jesus looked enviously at the figures hanging dead or nearly dead from the crucifixes, one after the other, marking the late hour with the long shadows they cast over the sand.

Just then, Jesus clutched himself, craning his head skywards, and cried up to the Heavens, "Eli, Eli, lema shamar?"[11] He splayed his body out upon a rock, as if to die by a stroke of the divine, but time passed ordinarily, wholly unresponsive to his plea. He lay there quivering, unsmote.

Hours upon hours did Jesus lie there, and finally his

---

[11] "My God, my God, why have you spared me?"

eyelids did close. I realized that it had been two full days without sleep for the Rabbi, and I stood there watchfully, letting him rest upon his rock.

Suddenly the ground began to shake, and the tremors lasted for long enough that the men and women hanging from their crosses started to cry out declarations about God.

Jesus awoke, too, long enough to witness a guard look up at the crucifixes and shake his head, saying, "Someone important must have died today, for the earth to shake so in anger."

"It is I," Jesus wanted to say, I could tell, but the heat of his flesh would have belied him.

Toward evening, the other eleven disciples came down to Golgotha, having heard at last the news of Jesus' salvation. "Where is he? Where is Jesus Christ, our Messiah?" they asked me, looking out onto the rows of the martyred.

He must have changed a great deal in a day. For they did not recognize him lying there with his eyes blissfully closed, peaceful in his sleep.

—

Apart from the Judas Scroll, there are few mentions of the prophet Jesus among the apocrypha, suggesting that his influence did not extend beyond the tribes of Israel. Unlike the Book of Jesus, which focusses exclusively on his teachings, the Scroll of Judas emphasizes the story of the prophet himself, and adds to our understanding of those teachings and the role of prophecy in the lives of the ancient Hebrews. Among the prophecies attributed to Jesus are the eschatological, end-of-days predictions that he shared in common with the Essenes (the subject of several other Dead Sea Scrolls). Little is known, though, about how Jesus believed the world would end, and where the souls would go when divorced from these bodies.

CHAPTER 4:

Jesus, Unforsaken

Suggestions for Class Discussion:

Why did Jesus believe that God was his Father, who wanted him publicly executed as a human sacrifice? And when it became clear that he would survive, why did he feel that remaining alive would diminish his holiness? What could a dead Jesus have left behind that a living Jesus could not?

CHAPTER 5

Joan of Arc, Patron Saint of Mothers and Soldiers

JOAN OF ARC (1412–1481), the patron saint of mothers and soldiers, began life as a peasant girl in the town of Domrémy, in the Lorraine region of Northeastern France, then under Burgundian control. As a young woman she had a vision of the Archangel Michael, whose voice commanded her to break the English siege of Orleans, and bring the Dauphin Charles VII to Reims for his coronation, which she accomplished at the tender age of seventeen.

Though she was captured by the Burgundian army in 1431 and handed over to the English, she was eventually ransomed by King Charles, returned to French territory, and forbidden ever to lead an army into battle again.

Joan of Arc went on to live a modest life as a musician in the court of King Charles, and through royal proximity, gained the necessary titles to mother three sons who would go on to become a pope, a king, and an emperor, though she never married.

The following text is excerpted from the writings of Jean d'Aulon, Joan's bodyguard and squire, and the source of much historical scholarship on the life of France's most revered saint. Historians of the Early Renaissance have suggested that, for all his medieval posturing about chastity and virtue, Jean d'Aulon reveals a fondness for his charge that goes beyond mere loyalty.

—

As a prophet, Joan's debut in French royal society began with the coronation of Charles VII at Reims. On that midsummer day in Reims Cathedral, under the oppressive glare of the rose window at full bloom with the sun at its zenith, she knelt near the altar in her shining white armor, carrying the flag of her country, at the feet of France's true and rightful sovereign, and declared, "Noble Prince, the will of God is now accomplished which had commanded me to raise the siege of Orleans, then to bring you to this ancient city of Reims in order to receive the holy consecration which proves you to be the true king to whom of sacred right belongs the Kingdom of France."[12] And the congregation wept with joy and cried out, "Noel! Noel!"

But a peasant girl in the court of the Loire Valley quickly became a mere novelty, her presence descending into something of a nuisance. True, she had once been the savior of France and had led its army to its first victory in generations, but they began to wonder, what *name* did she bear? What did she and the nobility have in common?

At twenty-four years old, Joan still wore her armor everywhere she went. She still heard voices. And she was

---

[12] Monahan, Michael. *My Jeanne D'Arc*. New York: The Century Company, 1928. Page 143.

still as pure as the day she was born. Her virginity, which had been painstakingly discussed, and proven, by France's clerical leadership, had formerly marked her as an emissary of God, but now simply branded her as an eccentric.

I flush with shame when I recall the insults heaped upon this hero of France when she visited the home of Jean Poton de Xaintrailles, one of her most loyal lieutenants, after the war. At a feast held in her honor, Xaintraille's wife turned and said to Joan, "You tell the future! What a marvelous diversion! You should come to our *chateau* next week and tell us which of us will have sons and which will have daughters." And this was the most idle of insults. To which Joan replied, most seriously, "But, Madame, you will have no heirs." Such truth had never before been uttered in the presence of a French noblewoman.

On another occasion, a group of younger nobles, merry with too much wine, put her to mockery for wearing men's clothing, in voices too loud to be ignored. Joan, in her disarming manner, replied, "Indeed, I wear a man's armor, and a man's *sword*," to which remark the men answered with a sober silence. But the one insult they all could agree upon—the great consensus among these nobles, many of whom owed their very lives to her—was that our Joan was unavailingly mad. As her squire and dutiful friend, I kept my silence but raged within myself: "If this is madness, then sanity is overrated!"

Charles VI, the late king of France and the father of Charles VII, believed that he was made of glass. He forgot his own name, assaulted his own soldiers, blew bubbles into his soup at dinner, and covered his body in a thick padding in case he should ever topple over. It was soon after he died that Joan began to hear the voice of the Archangel. Had the Angel been speaking to Charles as well? Perhaps the Archangel drove him mad to clear the way for her glorious ascendance?

It was the cruel memory of "Charles the Mad" that plagued Joan's own king, "Charles the Victorious." Many a night after the Loire Campaign had ended, and France restored to French rule, Charles sought comfort from The Maid of Orleans, who had helped obtain his victories through her very madness. "Young and of strong erotic proclivities, Charles had found himself magnetized by her charming, wholesome personality, even as his soul was subdued by the sense of her supernatural power."[13] But Joan of Arc prized her virtue above all else, for it had become the seal of her divine favor.

Yet rarely now did Joan resort to invoking God to chase the King out from her tent, as she had on certain nights on the march to Reims years ago, shouting at the naked monarch: "Allez vous-en! Le fils de Marie!" ("Get out of here! By the Son of Mary!") just as she had said to the English back in the city of Orleans.

Ever since he ransomed her from her Burgundian captors, the King and Joan of Arc had become close in a filial sense, with her ennoblement, and with the patronage of his mother-in-law, the Queen Yolande of Aragon, who treated Joan like a favorite daughter. And then there was the Duke d'Alençon.

If ever a man was suited to compromise the virtue of Joan, it was d'Alençon. They had fought side by side in the

---

[13] Monahan, Michael. *My Jeanne D'Arc*. New York: The Century Company, 1928. Page 129.

Battles of Jargeau, Beaugency, and Patay. She called him *le beau Duc*, and he knew her fondly as *la belle guerriere*. Indeed, he had the sort of roguish charm that good women everywhere seek to reform through their tender embraces. Tall and broad-shouldered, with well-cut features and a sculpted quality, he seemed out of place among the delicate nobility, and in fact, he had married into the royal family through Charles' sister, Jeanne de Valois. Joan of Arc and her Duke shared an outsider's awareness absent those forever confined within the circle.

And most pertinent of all, he possessed the libertine's wisdom for fine conversation, by which the heart of a maiden is earned. Whenever the Duke appeared at court, Joan could not contain a smile of relief that she would not spend the weekend yoked to a procession of dullards who spoke exclusively of God or war, the subjects for which she herself had grown justly famous, and which she therefore detested as dinner-table talk.

As France was once again in the hands of the French, and God besought her for nothing more glorious than an occasional prayer, in her newfound idleness, Joan would seek out the Duke at his palace, and stroll with him far outside the range of the windows of his estate.

"Archery is an English sport," the Duke complained, when Joan told him that she had taken up this pastime in her capacity as a gentlewoman.

"The day I concede that point is the day France forfeits the art of war to the English," she said.

"Take solace, *la belle guerriere*, in this: that the French are better horsemen," the Duke replied. "It is our nature to love living things." He gave a friendly wink and put on a mischievous smile—just the sort of gesture that The Maid abided from no one else.

"From your tongue, the most innocent words are befouled," she said, sympathetically. "I cannot help but read crudity into your character."

"The fault is yours, then," he said.

"When you speak of 'our nature,' surely you've neglected to mention that our nature is divine?"

"I couldn't agree more," the Duke answered with another comely smile, which once again had the effect of shuffling suggestively the meaning of the words just

PAGES from the TEXTBOOK of ALTERNATE HISTORY

uttered. "I suppose I should be careful not to take long walks with beautiful unmarried women," the Duke said. "Or . . . at least not when the Duchess is at home."

Joan slowed her pace and folded her hands, closing her eyes as though to show the depth of her faith. "My virtue has been tested so many times, I could be your guardian angel, defending your virtue against temptation. The Duchess should *thank* me for having you along."

At that, d'Alençon grew bold in a way to which only I, Joan's shadow, am privy to. "Won't you ever grow weary of virtue? It is well enough for a girl at war to be chaste, but a woman of your beauty ought to know the lover's embrace—and *her own child's* embrace—before death's."

"I *will* be a mother," Joan said, in the tone of knowing which she assumed when proclaiming a divine prophecy.

Joan of Arc once told Robert Baudricourt, the governor of Vaucouleurs, that she "would give birth to three sons: a pope, an emperor, and a king. In response to Baudricourt's gallant offer to father one of these illustrious offspring, Joan declined, saying, 'Gentil Robert, nennil, nennil, il n'est pas temps; le Saint-Esperit y ouvrera' [nay, nay, Master Robert, now is not the time; the Holy Spirit will see to it]. Baudricourt circulated the story of this conversation, zestfully relating it more than once in the presence of clergymen and nobles."[14]

Those, like myself, who knew Joan as more than a savior—as a person of common faults and common vulnerabilities—understood that as a young woman she had truly expected, waited, to become a mother and remain pure, in the divine pattern of the Virgin Mother. Her whole life it seems she had been waiting for the Archangel Michael—who had been her guiding light, who had put her through the trials of war and defeat and humiliation—to do more than speak to her. Even Mary was *touched* by the Archangel Gabriel, rather than *talked to*, and did Mary feel any different from how Joan felt, when His words first penetrated her?

The Duke, though, was only the catalyst that excited a deeper transformation within The Maid, one that changed

---

[14] Astell, Ann and Bonnie Wheeler. *Joan of Arc and Spirituality.* New York: MacMillan, 2003. Page 51.

her in her very core. The desire that he had stirred within her found no outlet in the life of the court—a life somehow both sterile and debauched—and Joan was soon possessed by a restlessness that she could neither name nor quench.

After years of striving for purpose among the purposeless, Joan announced that she would return to her family in Lorraine, whereupon she was bid farewell and departed with little fanfare, but received back into the little town of Domrémy like a queen.

She soon discovered that her childhood companions, her neighbors, even her family, had lived so long with the *legend* of Joan of Arc that they could no longer see her plainly. She decided to sojourn again, this time farther north, to Cambrai, where she pursued God with the same vigor and relentlessness with which she pursued the English armies not long ago.

I did not join her on this particular journey, but a piece of writing survives from her years of retreat into the monastic life: the "Apology to the Archangel Michael," which she wrote while studying scripture and music at Cambrai Cathedral:

The first place where I felt every stitch in the weave of my soul responding to the gravity of God was shivering from the granite tones of the pipe organ of Cambrai.

When I sat in the pews, there was a deathly silence, as of a man cupping his hands over my ears. I wondered for a moment if I had gone deaf—if God had taken away Your voice, and all other voices with it. I was like a newborn fascinated by its own powers of sense.

Then, "at the ringing of the angelus bells, at the very hour when the Ave Maria was being prayed in remembrance and renewal of the Annunciation,"[15] the first strains of that exquisite instrument were sounded. A dropping, heavy wind, from the ceiling down, like a spirit taking possession; then a light, lifting melody, as though a bird were pursuing the errant soul. The music surrounded me, vibrating in the stone, casting spears of light across my field of vision, pervading the very ether with tones that I could taste.

I admit that the glories of Cambrai Cathedral had not

---

[15] Astell, Ann and Bonnie Wheeler. *Joan of Arc and Spirituality*. New York: MacMillan, 2003. Page 69.

touched me at first. I had seen the great cathedrals of Orleans, Rouen, Reims, and Paris. Its flying buttresses, ionic columns, and all its grotesques had seemed to me simply another pattern in the great veil of the world that conceals the divine. Nothing in my sight had ever been sacred, it seemed to me then, and the more I witnessed, the more the scurf of the world merely yielded to the profane. It was only when I shut my eyes, and listened to Your voice, that I ever knew holiness. And then that day, in Cambrai Cathedral, when I heard that contradictory fugue, well, the revelation of music overwhelmed the revelation of voices, and drowned out its tyranny of endless meanings.

When it was finished, I will never forget, I was still on my knees, and I said to you, "Enough of this repenting."

Four years into her apprenticeship, Joan summoned me. I arrived at Cambrai after twilight, the night sky lit only by a wan crescent moon, hearing the same dulcet tones that had once inspired Joan as I approached the Cathedral. Only this time, as I passed under the threshold of God's house, and the setting of her new life was revealed to me, Joan herself sat at the organist's bench, mastering the pedal and key as though the instrument (and the church itself) were an extension of her body. Taking notice of my arrival, she descended and, as I made to kneel, lifted me into an embrace. We pulled away, and I gazed upon her.

It was the most startling transformation I have ever witnessed. Age was evident in her face now, in the most appealing way. Each crease described a habit of emotion that she could no longer mask with piety. Her aloof and sanctimonious stare was gone. In its place were eyes that searched, and found, another self within the other's gaze. She had become human in a way that would have been startling to those who sought to deify her, or to slander her. What war had wrought upon our Joan was nothing compared to the alchemy of time, music, and solitude.

Had these changes really taken place while living in the cold cellar of a church? I asked of her.

"No, Jean, God is more like a song than like a building. He does not sit by and wait to be crumbled, but is always moving in so many directions that you cannot locate Him and say *there is God*, yet you always know He is there."

Here again was Joan the prophet. In the most significant way, she remained unchanged.

She had summoned me to aide in her first mission since the liberation of France, which was to find the Duke d'Alençon, who was destined to father her children. My disappointment must have been visible, because Joan put her hands upon my shoulders and brought her face close to mine, just as she had done with La Hire, Xaintrailles, and d'Alençon before a great battle. Her sense of purpose shone from her eyes, as fervently as it had back then. I dared not question the resolve of this extraordinary woman to whom France owed her very existence.

With my limited powers of mind, I cannot fathom the agonies to which Joan must have submitted herself in order to reach this crisis. *La Pucelle*, defined by her virtue, yearned now to become a sinner, one of the despoiled, an animal like the rest of us.

She could not, as Mary had, be both mother and maiden. To fulfill her own prophecy, that she would give birth to a pope, an emperor, and a king, she had to sacrifice her virginity, her proof of divine favor.

Four leagues out from the Duke's palace, with dusk rapidly approaching, Joan halted our party and announced that we would set up camp where we stood. "*Le beau Duc* must come to me," she announced.

I wondered, was it prophecy or pride that caused this delay? Now that I had accommodated myself to my Lady's desires (however I may have disapproved), I simply wished for her to be fulfilled. I feared that Joan, forged in war, polished in court, and ensouled in the teachings of the church, might fail in love. But then, when he sent word that he would be arriving that morning, I remembered that Duke d'Alençon was a man, and untroubled by morality, undeterred by the coyness of her sex.

Before dawn, the Duke d'Alençon rode into our encampment, and dismounted before his gray steed had come to a full stop, which bespoke an eagerness, unseemly in a man of his position. The Duke strode forth with a swagger that struck me as undeserved, as though he were a boy playing at knighthood, about to be rewarded with a prize he neither earnestly sought nor fairly earned. But I will not deny Joan her love story, should she so wish to name it. As her sworn protector, I remained with her as the Duke entered the pavilion. I watched furtively as they smiled tears and whispered to each other, of what you and I will never know.

For all his gloating outside the tent, d'Alençon was skilled enough in love to treat his prize delicately, and the tiring business of removing her armor somehow maintained an innocent quality. Rather than displacing her breastplate first, d'Alençon occupied himself with all of the ties and buckles that bound her limbs in iron coils, keeping such steady eye contact that it must have been slightly burdensome, but perhaps hypnotic. I turned away at first, but, as the Duke d'Alençon fell short of my threshold of trust, I was obliged to watch.

The act itself was neither languorous and slow, nor quick and hungry, but conveyed an impression of two mountaineers climbing upward, hands always grasping for an edifice, with sudden pauses to give their straining limbs repose. Joan bled upon the greaves of her armor: for all their patience, they did not finish removing her leggings.

That night we imposed upon the Duke to stay in his

palace. D'Alençon somehow overcame his scruples and went to bed with his wife. As I tossed and turned in my own bed, not far from Joan's, my mind stirred with irony at the memory of Joan's *beau Duc* on the eve of their first battle, when he confided his fears about the superior numbers and training of the English. Joan had said, comfortingly, "Why do you fear, *gentil duc*? Have I not promised your wife to bring you back safe and sound?"[16]

Though such memories interfered with my sleep, moments later I had already descended into the cellars of dream, when I was rudely awakened by a light, blinding at first, then dissipating into its spectral elements, leaving behind the silhouette of three angelic figures. Though the scene was partly obscured by the curtain, and I lay delirious with night wakefulness, I saw the drifting forms advance like figures in a stained-glass window.

To this day, no man has ever borne witness to Joan's visions but I. They were beautiful and strange. They lent a pall to the atmosphere that was somehow frightening in its

[16] Monahan, Michael. *My Jeanne D'Arc*. New York: Century Company, 1928. Page 39.

capacity to comfort, instantly, all who fell under it. This was not the Archangel Michael, nor the saints Catherine and Margaret, all of whom had visited her before—but minor angels, strangers to Joan's pantheon of voices.

From my vantage, it appeared as though the seraphim were hovering above Joan's bed. They did not appear gentle and serene, but austere. In fact they glowed only faintly of God's reflected light, and each of them wore a stare that was studious, unfatherly.

Then they appeared, to my horror, to be inspecting her, lifting her sheets and reaching down to her prostrate body, widening the distance between her two ankles, bending her knees into a lurid pose. The scene was reminiscent of others endured by Joan—this hero of France!—so many times before. I saw it when Joan was "handed over to the Queen of Sicily, by whom The Maid was privately examined; and after examination made by the matrons, the lady stated to the King that she and the other ladies found most surely that this was indeed a true Maid."[17]

---

[17] Seguin de Seguin, qtd. in Marina Warner. *Joan of Arc: The Image of Female Heroism*. New York: Alfred A. Knopf, 1981. Page 16.

And again, when she was seized by the English, and subjected to "odious examinations calculated at least to humiliate her and break her nerve. Then the royal Bedford took the fore, ordering a further test, which in no way injured his victim, while it gave his name to eternal disgrace. For this exalted Englishman had taken care to have a peep-hole made in the wall, in order to gratify his noble curiosity."[18]

Now the angels. But, to their chagrin, Joan had donned her armor before bed, sleeping even in her padding and mail, and in their haste to investigate her fabled purity, they jostled her body, and she awakened. Perhaps the angels had believed, all this time, that Joan's armor was her chastity? Yet she proved, in thwarting their perverse design, that the white armor was not a badge of virtue, but a cross to ward off the cold gaze of ministering angels.

She spoke not a word, but rose from her bed, and though her height was unimposing, her eyes burned with that old fury which had sent so many Armagnacs to war,

---

[18] Monahan, Michael. *My Jeanne D'Arc*. New York: Century Company, 1928. Page 51.

and sent so many English soldiers to the grave. Then she cried out in a lion's voice to the Lord himself, asking why He sent such poor proxies, as though He were too brilliant to be gazed upon, and Joan drew her sword, and she chased His sexless kinsmen away.

—

True to her prophecy, Joan bore and mothered three great men: a pope, a king, and an emperor. But for all her sons' titles, which each of them received as an inheritance from France's savior, none of their accomplishments reached the heights of Joan of Arc's legacy, nor could ever displace her memory in that nation's history.

Though her children were born illegitimate, precluding *ipso facto* any claim to either virginity or fidelity, Joan was beatified by Pope Pius X in 1909 and canonized by Pope Benedict XV in the year 1920, which led to an opening up of sainthood to those holy women who had previously been regarded as sinful in the eyes of the church, merely for using the instruments that God gave them.

CHAPTER 5:

Joan of Arc, Patron Saint of Mothers and Soldiers

Suggestions for Class Discussion:

Why did all the men of France (and the angels in heaven) try so relentlessly to establish Joan's virginity? Was her *maidenhead* the savior of France? What, after all, are the genitalia of a saint, to God? How else could Joan have lived out her life, than in music? What do you do with the rest of your years, when you've already liberated your country and coronated the king at the age of seventeen?

CHAPTER 6

Columbus Discovers Asia

ACCOUNTS FROM THE EARLY EXPLORATION of Asia suggest that its discoverer, Christopher Columbus (1451–1506), had secretly imagined something different from what he had proposed to Ferdinand and Isabella. Though he had applied for a charter, and sponsorship, for the purpose of reaching Asia by a Western sea route—the feat for which he is known to history—from his private journal historians conclude that he hoped to discover an imaginary Atlantis resting between the continents that he called by the name of "America," the etymology of which we now believe derives from the Italian *Amare Cane*, or dog-love.

The following account was written by Bartolome De Las Casas, the grandson of Francisco De Las Casas, who accompanied Columbus on that first voyage.

—

There was no America. Only the Atlantic. A flat, blue surface folding over itself. No savages to subdue. No gold to mine. No islands of paradise, even. Columbus was chagrined by the ocean's vast emptiness. A great undiscovered continent was something he had imagined, and now all that was left for him to do was proceed toward the relative banality of Asia. But there would be gold and savages there, too, he told himself.

But how bitter that the prehistoric country of his dreams, and the civilizations he imagined there, would never be. A New Europe, a fresh start, and the continuance of his great voyage pushing west across the earth for hundreds of years without ever reaching its limit.

Columbus was not alone. Adventurous men traveled with him, men who had at times entertained thoughts of mutiny—not against their captains, not against the crown, but against Columbus himself.

Yet, as long as the rations held, he did not suffer insurrection, only ennui. For many days Columbus looked down at the surf crashing against the hull of the ship, speckled white, like a thirsty tongue. Occasionally, while staring into the water, Columbus would find himself feeling philosophical, and engage his fellow travelers with his *pensées*.

It was one such day. The Santa Maria, flanked by her two sisters, sailed headlong into the skyline. Another rotation of the sun had brought that nuclear light down to the horizon, and they coasted slowly toward it. Venus appeared like a mole in the sky's complexion, low and to the left, then suddenly all the stars emerged like a pox.

"Francisco," Columbus called to a mate, who stood only a few feet away and toward the bow, "why do you think, when the sun sets, the blue fades away from the water?"

"Water is reflective, like glass," Francisco said. "It looks blue to you because the sky is blue. Only when there is no light being reflected on it can you see its true color."

"But if there is no light, Francisco, then you can't see anything. It is just black."

Francisco nodded, the ends of his mustache twitching in the wind like an insect. "Wine-dark, sir, is what Homer called it."

On the morning of the seventh day of the third month after the voyagers' departure, the Santa Maria suddenly lurched and stalled, groaning with the burden of its weight, followed by the Pinta, then the Niña. No one had sighted land.

"Did anyone drop anchor?" Columbus called out. "Has anyone gone adrift?" The Admiral, when he arrived at his senses, answered that no man or anchor had been cast off.

Craning his neck over the bow, a lookout announced, "We've touched land!" But when Columbus looked out, he saw nothing.

"A sandbar," Francisco clarified.

"Then land must be near," said the Admiral, soberly, not wishing to excite the crew.

"Or," said Columbus, "the mountain ranges of some buried world," still dreaming.

When it turned out not to be an indication of land, nor the peak of some Atlantean wonder, the seamen had no other course but to extricate the ships from the ridge, by means of shifting all the weight to the bow, since they had already passed over a good part of the border, and raising their masts high to the wind. Turning their heads to where the ship left its wake, the men could see a blurred and corrugated orange stripe of sandbar stretching out like a seawall far to the north and the south, as if splitting the ocean in two.

"Has the Niña suffered any?" Columbus asked Francisco, who had started inspecting the Santa Maria for wood rot.

Rather than reply, Francisco handed Columbus the awl with which he had been testing the frame. "Why don't you make sure the crew is safe?"

Columbus wondered if he should have ordered the

Admiral to punish his insubordinate shipmate, for the sake of a well-ordered voyage, but decided instead to go into his stateroom and tinker with his astrolabe.

When the Santa Maria finally arrived in Shanghai, the Admiral raised the royal standard, and the other two ships bore the green cross with the insignia of the King and Queen. All the appropriate declarations were made, and three heathens were brought on board to be studied. These specimen were mere villagers, and had none of the ornament or riches that had been described in *The Travels of Marco Polo*. Somewhat disappointed, Columbus declared that, since the people of this country were not as Marco Polo had described, they must not be true Chinese. He ordered them detained and sent back to the kingdom, for examination. Their poverty was disconcerting, since the royal coffers were depleted, and rations were becoming scarce. Then he, Francisco, and the comptroller who had been appointed by the Crown all stepped out onto land, where fog moved downwind toward Portugal.

Walking through the streets of Shanghai, beside horses

and wagons drawn along on grooved paths, Columbus, Francisco, and the comptroller drew impolite stares and laughter. To the townsmen, they appeared funnily stretched, gangly-armed like monkeys, and ungracefully tall. They were unclean as only seamen can be, and even fishmongers held their noses as they passed.

Columbus approached a group of savages and attempted to barter broken bits of ceramic and glass for some pomegranates, but the merchant only stared vacantly at the fragments with which he was presented. The comptroller suggested to Columbus that there was perhaps a language barrier that had obscured his intentions.

When another customer squeezed in past them and laid down a slip of decorated paper, he walked away with a dozen pear-shaped fruit. Columbus was incredulous. Why did this merchant accept this useless bit of ornate parchment, covered with ink, while he wanted none of the treasures that they had brought from across the ocean? The merchant tucked his earnings away in a box with a complicated arrangement of drawers and compartments; then he clicked together some beads, laid out in a wooden frame connected by a beam and a series of rods, upon which several more beads were lanced.

Impatient, Columbus began to pantomime by rubbing his stomach, and pointing three fingers at his mouth. "We're hungry. Our men need food," he said, indicating his ship. "Is there anything we have that you would barter for?" With a sweeping gesture, he seemed to encompass his whole party.

We don't buy slaves here, the merchant said, shaking his head. *But what about your necklace? Is it gold?*

Seeing the merchant pointing at his crucifix, Columbus shielded it by taking the medallion in his fist. "Does no one know Christ in this country? Are *all* men godless in China?"

Francisco leaned in close to Columbus. "Your men are hungry. The Lord Jesus Christ would feed them if it cost a hundred medallions."

Columbus stood motionless in the mist. Finally, the comptroller spoke. "Señor Columbus, the court will gladly reimburse you for whatever costs are incurred in service of your function."

Columbus unlatched the necklace, handing it over. The merchant tested its weight, examined its sheen, and took one arm of the cross into his teeth. Columbus made as though to draw his musket. Francisco held his arm.

This is no good. Not even twenty-four karats. The merchant handed back the medallion, and turned his attention to the next customer. Columbus stared down at the lump of gold in his hand.

The last entry in Columbus' journal reads: "the natives of this land appear to have no religion. If we could Christianize them, they would make good servants. With fifty men, I could conquer the whole of them, and govern them as I pleased."

—

This account of Columbus' voyage is the only extant record to attempt to construct the events leading up to the Shanghai mutiny. It is offered as one explanation of why the continents eventually ceased contact, and how Europe came to be called "New America."

CHAPTER 6:

Columbus Discovers Asia

Suggestions for Class Discussion:

What would the effect have been if the first contact between New America and China had been made by sages, rather than merchants? Why did Columbus believe that paradise could be found in the middle of the ocean? If Columbus were successful in subduing China and populating the land with Christians instead of Confucians, how would things be different?

CHAPTER 7

John Smith is Hanged for Treason

IN 1606, Edward Maria Wingfield (1550–1631), the man
who would eventually lead the Jamestown Colony to
become the first successful colony in the New World, was
almost deposed by the rascal John Smith (1580–1606).

Though in his short life John Smith did not achieve any
of his extraordinary ambitions, after his death among his
papers was found a journal in which he had written a
lengthy fictional account of his imagined future exploits.
This serial novel, *The Adventures of John Smith in Indian*

Country, was published posthumously, surviving for centuries as a children's classic, and is thought to have influenced the adventure stories of later American writers James Fenimore Cooper and Washington Irving, though Smith himself never set foot on American soil.

The following account was written by Neville Shaw, who was on the ship with Smith when he was hanged.

—

John talked of being saved by a beautiful woman. Sometimes it was on a beach, after having drifted ashore from a shipwreck. Sometimes it was in the woods, after being felled by an arrow wound, then tended to health again by the gentle care of a beautiful squaw. Then, there was his Indian princess fantasy. There was always his Indian princess fantasy.

Now we were preparing to waylay the three ships of the Virginia Company in an island of the Carribeans, with the express purpose of hanging the yeoman Smith, who had proven himself not only a rascal, but an emerging threat to the voyage. His conspiracy consisted mostly of boasts. He had at one time or another claimed he could do something better than each of the other hundred and one men on board, including, fatally, the job of Captain Newport.

By nature imaginative, John thought often about his own death. When applied to the circumstances of his own end, his imaginings were intricate and endless. He saw himself cast overboard and drowning in the Atlantic. He saw his body speared through by an Algonquin arrowhead. But never did he envision himself dangling from the gallows, his body left to the scavenging birds of an uninhabited island thousands of miles from his homeland.

This I know, because I was assigned to be his keeper—as the only man on board who could bear to listen to Smith prattle and whine drunkenly about life's vicissitudes. And in those last days, his prattling consisted mostly of fantasies about women and death. Then eventually, only death.

In April of 1607 we made land, which we dubbed Cape Henry. A few dozen men disembarked for the island, and set immediately to constructing their habitat. After they finished, they would gather wood to make a fire, then tie off the noose with which to hang the mutineer.

From the port of the ship where Smith was shackled, he watched the construction of the sad edifice which was to be his gallows. The men were half-finished erecting the instrument of his undoing, when night fell like a toppling wall. And still, Smith stood helplessly chained, thirsty and weary to the point of delirium.

Something stirred us awake. A sound, which might have been the warbling of strange birds, or insects, or animals, so foreign was the land to our ears. I stepped out of the ship's cabin and, in the wan light of a lantern, saw a blurred frenzy on the shore, and could barely even make out the despicable face of John Smith only ten feet away, which was fixed in a state of either ecstasy or confusion.

"Do you know that sound? Those are your countrymen being slaughtered by savages!" I shouted at him.

He said, in a strained whisper, which is all he could muster, "Saved by Indians. Saved by Indians."

"Not saved, *slaughtered*!" I said. But John Smith could not be corrected, even by his own naked ears.

By morning, the mood was changed. Seven of our men had been cast into the ocean, and others suffered wounds which would lead to the same fate, but none of the savages had been captured, and there was no one left to punish. No one, that is, but the rascal Smith.

So the gallows served as a reminder of our purpose for landing—that the whole episode was the fault of one man, and that man, when he came to witness what evil his mutiny had wrought, did naught but smile and gloat.

But the air was thin with grief, and the spirit with which the execution proceeded was not of revenge, but duty.

From ship to shore, Smith walked the final walk—the walk dividing men from ghosts. As he stepped off the ship onto land, there was a momentary surge of tender feeling as his boot touched down on the soft sand—the yielding of earth, unlike the textures of life aquatic, the invulnerability of anchor, wheel, and wood. In another life, Smith might have been an honorary savage, following the Indians into the forest and becoming their champion. But he had not yet fulfilled his ambitions for *this* life, much less the next. He could not imagine doing anything partially; it is his curse.

He mounted the stairs, taking each heavily, not with his usual brisk stride, yet with his chin jutting proudly into the air. Then, the fifth stair—that would be pulled away.

There stood John Smith, defiantly looking out from the gallows, next to the noose from which he was to be hanged. Stripped of everything else to his name, Smith kept his vigilance. It was clear, from his eyes, that he, unlike many another condemned man, had spirit left to squander on rage. "We are already at war!" he cried. "And we have yet to reach the continent."

"*We* are at war," said Wingfield, who, by a draw of names, was charged with removing the board and ushering in the death of John Smith, "but *you* have only the pit."

"Isn't there any common sense amongst you? We *must* open the Virginia Company's instructions to find out what our duties are in the New World; without leadership, we are doomed to suffer another ruinous attack!"

The response from the crewmen was a stricken and superstitious silence. Wingfield turned toward Captain Newport. "Traitor though he is, we must heed John's point here," he said. "What say you, Captain?"

The Captain tried to raise his eyes to where Wingfield and Smith stood, but to do so would have been to face the glare of the sun crowning over the trees behind them. So he looked down at the sand as he spoke. "We were told not to break the seal on the Virginia Company's orders until we reached the Americas. But we have made land, for better or worse, and are much in need of laws."

Captain Newport broke the seal and opened the paper containing his employer's directives. On it were listed the names of the seven governors of what was to become the colony of Jamestown. Watching this, I thought momentarily of Walter Raleigh, who was sentenced so many times to death, but somehow emerged each time unscathed, and always with funding to launch another foolhardy voyage into the heart of darkness. Raleigh had been inspiration for Smith, of course, but never moreso, I supposed, than at that moment.

"Christopher Newport . . ." The Captain. *There* was no surprise. "George Kendall . . . Bartholomew Gosnol . . ." Men of family. The gathered murmured their approval.

"John Percy . . . John Ratliff . . . John Martin . . ." The

name "John" here, spoken thrice, was like the lashing of a whip to us, which struck the air but never broke the skin.

"And . . . Edward Wingfield, who is here designated to be the colony's commander and president."

Smith, disappointed but not surprised to hear his name unannounced, let go, finally, of the rage, letting it seethe until it turned cold with all of nature's indifference.

President Edward Wingfield, in his first act as president of Jamestown, announced the verdict on John Smith: "John Smith of Willoughby, for your treachery to the King and the Captain Christopher Newport, you are hereby sentenced by His Majesty's authority to be hanged from the neck until dead. Do you have any last words?"

Then, to our surprise, rather than one last vainglorious attempt at fame in an oration to the men of Jamestown, Smith leaned over to Wingfield and whispered something in his ear. Years later, after the settlement of Jamestown was no longer uncertain, and his notoriety in England renowned, Wingfield confessed to me the final words of the rascal John Smith: "No matter what you do for the colony, it is the land that will decide her fate. The only thing you can do is to live openly and inspire men; you cannot direct history; you can only act your part."

Perhaps this is why Smith acquiesced so readily to the noose; he was secure in the knowledge that he fulfilled his role as rouser and mutineer to the best of his powers. Or perhaps Master Wingfield betrayed the truth in order to preserve Smith's honor, and what the rascal really said was, "Are there Indian princesses in heaven"?

—

Shaw devotes much of the rest of his account to Smith's literary legacy. John Smith's posthumous success as a writer of tall tales, and his legend as a charismatic troublemaker, were more significant to the shaping of a nascent America than they have been to the literature of England, and for that reason it is fitting that so many American stories refer back to the sad tale of John Smith and his failed mutiny. The first American novelist never arrived in America.

CHAPTER 7:

John Smith is Hanged for Treason

Suggestions for Class Discussion:

Smith hoped to be named as one of the governors of the colony, but the Virginia Company did not see Smith as fit; what would have changed were Smith to survive and help run the Virginia Colony? Novel writing was a rare undertaking in the Seventeenth Century; if Smith *had* survived, would historians have mistaken his stories for historical accounts? Might they have mistaken *The Adventures of John Smith in Indian Country* for fact?

Ben Franklin, Clergyman

REVEREND   BENJAMIN   FRANKLIN   (1706–1790),
American preacher, theologian, and longtime Presbyterian
minister of the Massachusetts Bay Colony, was born into
humble circumstances. As the child of Josiah Franklin, a
tithingman in the Presbyterian Church, Benjamin was an
ideal candidate to fill the increasingly populist function of
pastor to Boston's ministry during the Great Awakening.

Cotton Mather, the famous Massachusetts minister and
barrister during the Salem witch trials, personally

cultivated Benjamin Franklin and brought him into the ranks of Harvard College, seeking through his budding brilliance to oppose and unseat President Leverett and his liberal policies from the College. His father, Increase Mather, had been president of Harvard a generation earlier, and both men exerted an influence over the board of the College disproportionate to their minor official duties.

Mather's collected writings, excerpted here, include a lengthy defense of Franklin and his role in the controversial early years of his development as a clergyman, and as a divinity student at Harvard College.

—

Reverend Franklin was ordained at Holden Chapel in a modest ceremony surrounded by his classmates. Following as it did the commencement of his class, the sun had already downed, and tallow candles were lit throughout the nave, as though we were gathered to honor the dead.

As I began the prayer, lowering the anointing oil to Franklin's brow, he winced, fleetingly, as though the touch about to be bestowed upon him were not of God, but of hellfire. It was only a flutter of the eyelid, but the implications were deep.

Years before, when he entered school at age fifteen, Ben Franklin was not the youngest, smartest, or most pious boy at Harvard College, but he was, by his own admission, the most obnoxious. And it must be said that at Harvard he faced much competition for the title. Yet I saw early on that the boy's innate talent, and his habit of self-discipline, made his constant and restless activity tolerable. He would soon, I anticipated, become the brand with which the hand of God would set Harvard College aflame.

In 1720, Benjamin's mother and father were persuaded to part with him, with the understanding that, as the top student at the Boston Latin School, he would be offered a stipend for living expenses. Their concern had been that Ben showed none of the temperament of a clergyman, and though they desired most ardently for him to join the clergy, were uncertain of the value of the ministry upon such a wasted soul. We assured them that we had made devout Christians out of harder men than Ben Franklin.

In fact, young Ben's training in piety was softer than most. His restlessness and curiosity ensured that we could not depend on the forceful hand of a father, but must coax him into God's grace as a mother into a loving embrace, meeting his skeptical nature at every turn with a gentle disposition and kind entreaties. For, though history has made a legacy of my obstinancy in the defense of God, and a marginal role in a trial against a bevy of wicked children, since my Salem days I have had fifteen children of my own, and by the time I met young Franklin I was painfully experienced in the iron will of adolescence, and the futility of beating thereon.

The first image I had of Ben Franklin the Harvard divinity student encapsulated, for me, his very nature. His best clothes had not yet arrived, and so he travelled in his working clothes, dirty at the knees and elbows, his pockets full to bursting with extra undergarments. On his way, he had stopped by the baker's and, not taking into account the price difference, asked for a three-penny loaf, of which they had none. Asking then for any quantity of bread that a three-penny piece would purchase, he was handed a single morsel of biscuit, which he handled delicately as he strode into the Yard, as though it weighed a stone.

I caught sight of him from the window of Harvard Hall, which contained the library, and, looking up from my French translation of Calvin's *Secret Providence*, I saw in Franklin a young man so intent on relishing his tiny morsel of bread, he might have been a papist altar boy who had gone without breakfast, taking his communion wafer.

When his baggage arrived from the other side of the Charles, and his considerable personal library moved into his dormitory, Franklin could be seen running to and fro across the green, heaving piles of books in a wheelbarrow, like a farm hand gathering wood for a fire. So that his industry stood on display for the entire school, and the picture so solidified him for his peers, that the image of Ben Franklin towing a wheelbarrow full of books became symbolic shorthand for the speed and efficiency with which he rose to the top of his class, and to a position of influence within the College in a single year.

At the time, young Ben would often speak wistfully

about his favorite fantasy—forging his own path, becoming a self-made man in some distant town, and disappearing from Harvard for good. I had known students to toss up their hands and go back to their lives as laborers, or as children of good name, but never one who excelled as effortlessly as did Franklin. It was as though he secretly sought, not escape from the ministry, but some alternative society that existed only in his imagination—some dream that he followed like a candle in the darkness, though when he drew too near, it scalded him.

That winter there was a fire in Harvard Hall. A log fire, left overnight from a meeting of the General Court, spread to the floor beams of the library, and was driven by the wind to the curtains; in a matter of minutes, it was consuming all in a great inferno. We—council members, faculty, students alike—stood around the Yard contemplating the hellish light it cast on the dark winter morning. Yet, for the pragmatist in our ranks, the fire did not conjure lofty musings of the Divine will, but began stirring up thoughts of a different sort—of "forming a company for the more ready extinguishing of fires, and mutual assistance in removing and securing the goods when in danger"[19] for the College. Later, he foreshortened the name to simply "an Engine Company."

Soon, Franklin's zeal for an Engine Company itself took on the consumptive power of a conflagration. He wrote in the *Gazette* about the need for such a service, both in his editor's column, and in letters from a dozen different voices, using characters of his own invention. He recruited nearly all the students in his class as volunteers, and even involved members of the community. Not content with bringing together the first Company for the purpose of extinguishing fires, Franklin decided that, in place of the private library of Harvard Hall, what the College needed was a subscription library to which the public contributed, and of which the public could also be beneficiaries.

Many of the faithful have asked me why, at this point, I did not openly oppose the liberalizing influence of Franklin on campus, so in chorus with the empty secularizing of its President Leverett. The truth is that, having brought

---

[19] Franklin, Benjamin. *The Autobiography of Benjamin Franklin.*

Franklin in under my auspices, I saw his notoriety as adding to my cause, and I saw the growing civic movement as yet another audience prone to our divine influence. It has been my error, I am often told, to rely on the credulity of the crowd. But I had always known men in the midst of a herd to be pliable, and why should I have thought that the followers of Franklin were any different?

Though as a student of religion Franklin was mediocre, his tendency to lead others into action made him an ally against evil. Even as he faltered in his efforts to penetrate the tower of Christian theology, he continued to dwell in the houses of labor. His presence uplifted the College; his sense of duty was infectious. My work was to steer his industry toward God's path. I began where I saw the greatest need: unseating the secular President Leverett. In my conversations with Franklin, I warned him against Leverett, defining him as someone who speaks the opposite of what he means, and who can never be trusted, for he is a skeptic who doubts God's word.

Franklin came face-to-face with Leverett once, though I

heard about it only afterwards. The boy had, I am told, constructed what he called a "battery"—a vessel that stored latent energy in physical form—and in a mood of mischief, lined up his classmates and had them touch it, sending a stimulating shock through the row. An older boy, embarrassed to have been a part of the spectacle, accused Franklin of bewitching him, and brought his activities to the attention of President Leverett. But the President was not compelled to act against Franklin until, months later, he received a letter from Abbé Nollet describing the boy's experiments with a steel rod, which sought to redirect lightning away from the steeple, out of his dormitory window. Nollet's complaint was that Franklin sought to control God's fury and devastation, and to conceal His glory. The letter claimed that "the lightning rod was an offense to God."[20] It was to this charge, and its intimations of scandal, for which Franklin finally had to answer.

Young Franklin sat waiting, so I presume, in Leverett's office, unattended. The chairs, the desk, the floors were all an even tone of darkness. Bits of light from the afternoon

---

[20] Abbé Nollet, qtd. in Isaacson, Walter. *Benjamin Franklin.*

glinted between the shadows cast from the window. He would have made the boy wait for what seemed like an hour, with no glass of water, nothing to read.

Then the president, John Leverett, would have entered from a side door, to show the student that he had been in his office all along, but merely occupied with matters more pressing than a boy's misbehavior.

"What's this I hear about Abbé Nollet?" he said simply. "Something about experiments with a lightning rod?"

"The Abbé speaks as though it is presumption in man to propose guarding himself against the thunders of Heaven!" Franklin said emphatically. "Surely the thunder of Heaven is no more supernatural than the rain, hail or sunshine of Heaven, against the inconvenience of which we guard by roofs and shades without scruple."[21]

"I wish you'd told me before that you were conducting experiments." The President's tone was neutral, so that Franklin could only guess at the implication. "I hadn't known that you possessed a keen scientific sense."

"You don't disapprove?" Franklin asked cautiously.

---

[21] Benjamin Franklin, qtd. in Isaacson, Walter. *Benjamin Franklin.*

"To have raised the ire of a French monk, and in your second year of study, a boy of barely sixteen years—this is a rare achievement."

Franklin paused in surprise, expecting anything but flattery. "My research so far is inconclusive," he began, "though the great and holy Reverend Cotton Mather has translated my preliminary findings into French and distributed them widely."

"Yes," Leverett said, "the great and holy Reverend is good at disseminating ideas."

I can only speculate, at that point, that President Leverett began to speak ill of me, and my influence upon the College, because Franklin insisted that the President's words did not bear repeating. But the conclusion was that Franklin began to study under Leverett's protégé, John Winthrop. The very name roils my stomach and raises my bile. Whereas his grandfather and namesake had been the very torch of Christian piety, young John Winthrop had become so "science-minded" that he had come to represent the next generation of cold secularization, molded after the example of impious men such as John Leverett.

God's work for me was clear. I arranged a debate between Winthrop and Franklin upon an issue for which I knew them to be in opposition: the use of spectral evidence. Franklin the pragmatist had at first been stubbornly against the use of visions and divine insight as evidence in a court, but after I had painted a vivid picture for him of the hellish condition of the Salem girl Betty Parris while in the throes of a spectre, his opinion changed, and he soon became the most eager convert to our cause. Franklin was, in the end, still a boy, and privy to the wisdom of his elders.

The debate was held in Holden Chapel, with all the boys from Franklin's class in attendance and, as I made sure, only a few from Winthrop's. The dusty light warmed the stone floor, and the echoes of adolescent voices rang out from every wall, then was gradually silenced. The participants of the debate stood at opposite sides of the chapel, at wooden lecterns, and wore the robes and wigs of their respective Halls.

Winthrop, speaking first, laid out his case with professional ease. Lifting his arms up incredulously, bringing them down on the lectern emphatically, gesturing open-handed toward the audience, posing rhetorical questions sneeringly in the direction of his opponent. When he finished, he had not only established that the use of spectral evidence in legal proceedings was inadmissable, but that it was reckless, and dangerous to the laws upon which the Empire was founded.

Franklin, after a pause that might have been mistaken for speechlessness, stepped forward and said, "What happens to a society in which a legal authority cannot trust the testimony of its members?" He let the air settle for a moment. "If your neighbor speaks to you about a personal experience, will you declare him a liar simply because you have not had the same experience? No. And should the courts behave any differently from the good citizen?

"We cannot deny our own sensory experience on the basis of probability, nor can we deny the sensory experience of others on such bases. We may seek an explanation, we may argue about its origins, but to preclude any spectral evidence whatsoever on the basis of its internal and unverifiable nature—we might as well prohibit expressions of opinion."

He did not address the question of the absolute truth of spectral evidence, nor the existence of the supernatural, but merely brushed the matter aside as irrelevant to proof, and said, in effect, "on to more important things." Certainly I, who had been making a case for the admission of spectral evidence for years, did not expect such a coup. My own arguments came out of the vividness of the picture drawn, the complexity of the scenes, which in all their specificity and depth *must* conform to some external reality. But the brilliance, the audacity, of Franklin was that he could, expanding on my example, use reason to disprove the notion of truth itself.

The debate proceeded thus: Winthrop would raise a point, subject it to logic, and in so doing, assert its proof; then Franklin would declare that point irrelevant, address the issue in the abstract, and cleverly assert the uncertainty of knowing either way for sure. He had come, at last, to his life's purpose: using the art of persuasion to return the faithful to God. I could not help myself—sitting up in the back of the chapel, I wept. Oh, Ben Franklin. God's Trojan horse at Harvard College!

What I perceived at first to be a resounding victory, however, sprung back upon us when President Leverett, who had sneaked in during the proceedings and sat in the rear pew, at the end walked up to the lectern beside Franklin and pronounced that he, as Harvard's new oratorical champion, would next month be travelling to the Collegiate School of Connecticut at Sayville (colloquially referred to as "Yale") to debate its own star divinity student, Jonathan Edwards.

The Sayville School had recently been founded in solidarity with our church's protest of the secularizing of Harvard College, and it promised to be an institution of faithfulness and devotion to God. I hesitated to send our most eloquent orator to challenge the piety of Mr. Edwards, especially given Franklin's tendency toward "free-thinking."

Furthermore, the subject of the debate was to be God's judgment, a topic on which I knew Franklin to be recalcitrant. The notion of a vengeful and jealous God did not catch with Franklin the pragmatist. This was our greatest point of contention. He was also hesitant to denounce false religions. Even the Quakers, whose many heresies brought about their exile from the colony, were, in Ben Franklin's view, also followers of Christ. He did not say as much to me, but I would not be surprised to learn that Ben Franklin did not believe in the devil at all.

It was our first blessing that the debate would be held in Sayville, far from the impressionable Bostonians who filled our pews, where it would not stain the reputation of Franklin in our own ministry. The journey by foot would take nearly a fortnight. By ship, it was two full days' travel. When we saw the modest wooden houses outlining the town, and the single wooden building of the college, sided with clapboard, and the abundance of trees, my sense of foreboding was diminished. Without scrutinizing my fellow traveller, I knew that, as he looked upon the sight, his mind turned to thoughts of how Yale could use the services of an Engine Company.

Our next blessing came in the form of the rector of the Sayville School, Timothy Cutler, who had graduated Harvard College fifteen years earlier, and was formerly a member of my church, now a preacher himself. He greeted us warmly, and invited us to supper, on the night before the great debate. Though his impeccable courtesy was, all the evening, tainted by an attitude of smugness that suggested that he knew beforehand how the days ahead would all unfold.

On the floor of Yale's "college house" sat not only the students, but more than a few significant figures from the Connecticut Colony, including Governor Saltonstall and Governor Elihu Yale himself. It was as though, improbably, the college had prepared itself for their annual commencement ceremony, rather than the tired polemics of two snivelling, but well-trained, boys. They had great faith in their lion Jonathan Edwards, and for good reason. And they wished, perhaps, to bear witness to the fall of Harvard College, with the symbolic rise of their own constellation.

My interest in this venture, as Leverett well knew, was split. I had no wish to see Franklin's religious tolerance take the day, but neither did I wish to watch my budding protégé fail. But most of all, I wished not to be associated with the spectacle, and not to have my reputation sacrificed at the altar of Harvard College.

The scene was reminiscent of a bout. Because of the tightness of the quarters, they stood nearly arm to arm, backlit by a large central window, so that, at every gesture, their shadows on the platform seemed to be colliding. Furthermore, Yale had not yet developed the sense of ceremony that pervaded Harvard College, so that neither speaker was expected nor desired to wear a wig or gown.

Our final blessing, perhaps, was that our Benjamin Franklin was no match as an orator for Jonathan Edwards, the true firebrand. Edwards began in an almost incantatory whisper, so that the audience had to lean forward, then built up his voice into thunderous claps. The effect, in fact, was so visceral that members of the crowd began to hold their stomachs and rock back and forth, or fall upon the ground and weep.

"The God that holds you over the pit of hell, much as one holds a spider, or some loathsome insect over the fire, abhors you, and is dreadfully provoked: his wrath toward you burns like fire; he looks upon you as worthy of nothing else, but to be cast into the fire; he is of purer eyes than to bear to have you in his sight; you are ten thousand times more abominable in his eyes, than the most hateful enomous serpent is in ours."[22]

What, indeed, could Franklin say to this evocation of God's will? He spoke evenly and rationally about the God of good works—how we can know nothing of God absolutely, but can guess only at His wishes, and that we can say nothing with surety but that God has equipped man to value good works on earth.

But the crowd was held in thrall by the inflamed words of their local hero. As Franklin spoke, they merely bided their time for another glorious assault upon their souls.

"O sinner! Consider the fearful danger you are in: it is a great furnace of wrath, a wide and bottomless pit, full of the fire of wrath, that you are held over in the hand of that God, whose wrath is provoked and incensed as much against you, as against many of the damned in hell. You

---

[22] Edwards, Jonathan. "Sinners in the Hands of an Angry God."

hang by a slender thread, with the flames of divine wrath flashing about it, and ready every moment to singe it, and burn it asunder; and [. . . there is] nothing that you ever have done, nothing that you can do, to induce God to spare you one moment."[23]

Franklin's final sally was, to my surprise, and that of the entire crowd there arrayed, to simply shake his head and laugh, loud and unrestrained.

The audience muttered indecisively, unsure whether the laughter was an indication of his obvious defeat, or of scorn.

But instead of ceding the floor or digging in to his opponent, Franklin decried the institutions of learning which had created them both. He took aim, in particular, against the rich parents who, burdened with children, "send them to the Temple of Learning, where, for want of a suitable Genius, they learn little more than how to carry themselves handsomely, and enter a Room genteely (which might as well be acquired at a Dancing-School), and from whence they return, after abundance of trouble

---

[23] Edwards, Jonathan. "Sinners in the Hands of an Angry God."

and Charges, as great Block-heads as ever, only more proud and self-conceited."[24]

And, fortune of fortunes, the chorus erupted into laughter, and the laughter infected the gallery, and soon Edwards himself could not resist the wave of levity that crashed over the room. Franklin had somehow struck a nerve more powerful even than Edwards' fires of hell. His voice had become the calm and level stream that extinguished it.

Although in the end he had taken the wind out of Edwards' powerful oratorical advantage and recovered his dignity, on the road home Franklin was troubled. I consoled my student by reminding him that it was no one's expectation that he would actually win the debate, given the venue and the elder boy's greater experience. President Leverett had trapped him, tried to make a fool of him, but he had somehow salvaged his pride, and emerged the better

---

[24] Benjamin Franklin, qtd. in Morison, Samuel Eliot. *Three Centuries of Harvard: 1636–1936.* Cambridge, MA: Harvard University Press, 1936. Page 61.

contender. He should be proud of his performance, and unashamed in the face of his critics.

But, Franklin said, looking up at me with changed eyes, it was not that he feared the loss to his earthly reputation, but that he had come to fear God's judgement. There in Yale's college house, a modest wooden building with small leaded windows, standing shoulder to shoulder with Edwards, Franklin had experienced a painful revelation. He could not efface the image of hell in his mind. He understood now that he was merely an insect held over a fire by an angry and whimsical god. The pit awaited him, unless he repent, and kneel, and renounce his skeptical and freethinking ways, and turn his thoughts forever upon God.

The flame of heaven had caught Franklin by the cloth, and the fire was spreading.

—

Though the Reverend Benjamin Franklin helped further scientific knowledge and civic institutions in several different areas, he is notable most of all for his influence upon the culture as a whole.

The effect of his extraordinary life is more elusive than that of a statesman or inventor, but also more pervasive and unmistakable. Benjamin Franklin has become the model for the American type: ascetic, pious, selfless, and modest to a fault.

Without Benjamin Franklin's example, the Founding Fathers would have been less concerned with the obligations of man toward God, and more concerned with the inherent "rights" of man. Instead of a document establishing the duties of each citizen to the Almighty, there might have been a document detailing government's duties to the individual. We may have even followed the misguided doctrine of Roger Williams, and removed the role of a church in American government altogether. In fact it is not too vast a claim to make, in the instance of Benjamin Franklin, that he was the man most responsible for shaping the American character, and its status, forever, as a Christian nation.

CHAPTER 8:

Ben Franklin, Clergyman

Suggestions for Class Discussion:

It was not reason, but imagination, that persuaded Ben Franklin of the reality of hell; what does it say about logic, that it became a barrier between the Reverend Franklin and his great revelation? Even before his conversion, Benjamin Franklin believed in God; why was Cotton Mather so determined that he believe in the devil too?

CHAPTER 9

Napoleon Invades Louisiana

NAPOLEON BONAPARTE, Emperor of West America, nearly lost his colonial empire when his navy was threatened by a slave revolt in the colony of Saint-Domingue ("Hayti," to the locals). It was only by the means of an alliance with their leader, the former slave Toussaint L'Ouverture, that Napoleon was able to invade Louisiana and establish West America, keeping his continental colonies from being sold off to East-American President Thomas Jefferson.

Hayti was the largest producer of cane sugar in the world, and Napoleon's most treasured property. That it was led by a charismatic former slave who rivalled Napoleon in his military prowess, and who had the effrontery to declare his slaves freemen and draft a constitution for Hayti, was an insult he bore fitfully. Forced to tolerate Toussaint's leadership during the Battle of New Orleans, Napoleon was already at work plotting his undoing.

Napoleon's brother-in-law, a mulatto by the name of Castaigns (husband of the Empress Josephine), was sent along with another brother-in-law, General Leclerc (husband of the Empress Pauline), to recruit Citizen-General Toussaint to help the French navy take control of Louisiana. The following account is compiled from Castaign's correspondence with his wife Josephine.

—

The members of the council on Saint-Domingue stood in a line leading from the office of the Consul Napoleon Bonaparte, snaking around its marble columns, through the palace garden, and terminating in the stables outside where the pungent smell of manure filled their delicate noses. These men were arrayed before the Emperor-to-be to praise him on his judicious decision to betray and murder the captain of Hayti's army and a citizen of the French Republic, Toussaint L'Ouverture.

The day before, Brigadier-General Vincent Ogé had had the audacity to dispute Consul Bonaparte's decision, going so far as to declare, "The end of Toussaint will mean the end of the Republic." Ogé was a man of military distinction, and regarded Toussaint's service as a citizen-general to be unassailable. His argument, expressed shakily but with admirable vigor at the last meeting of the council, was that a government with integrity could not sustain betrayals of its military leadership. His true feeling, as I well knew, which went unspoken that day, was that if France were to attack Hayti, France would lose.

Napoleon, who derived much political power from the loyalty of the army, could not remove or dishonor Ogé in plain view of an audience, but for all his seeming humility and quiet consideration, all present could see the Consul

Bonaparte's seething brain beneath the skin of his brow, as though, when the Consul contracts a fever, it is the rest of France that shivers from the ague.

So to salvage his pride, the Consul commanded every other councillor to line up in front of his palace and thank him. And one by one, the councilmen waddled forward into the great hall of the future Emperor, hanging their heads as though waiting for the blade of a guillotine to fall.

If Ogé failed to convince Napoleon of the rightness of supporting Toussaint, at least he persuaded him of its utility. Toussaint may have been the leader of a slave revolt, brashly drafting a constitution on behalf of men who were officially the property of France, but he was also a general of uncanny talent. Such men had a use, at least, in times of war.

Napoleon needed no reminding as to Toussaint's skill as a strategist. It had recently been implied by Beauchamp, in a book on Hayti, that Napoleon the tactician was second only to Toussaint, and that he had in fact borrowed many of his most ambitious military maneuvers therefrom.

"Toussaint's performance was such that, in a wider sphere, Napoleon appears to have imitated him."[25]

And in the estimation of the world, Napoleon was said to possess a *jealousy of power which made rival greatness intolerable.* "With an evil eye, therefore, did he regard the high position obtained by Toussaint L'Ouverture through his wise and generous efforts in the French colony of Saint Domingo. The brilliancy of his own fame seemed dimmed in his eyes by the glory achieved by a negro chieftain who had been a slave."[26]

So it befell that I was sent, along with General Leclerc, Brigadier-General Ogé, and twenty thousand soldiers, across the Atlantic Ocean to the shores of Saint-Domingue, to bring the unruly sheep back into France's flock. But, buying time with our advance, arriving at Port-au-Prince suddenly, without warning, and with a navy readied for war, we purchased too, with our haste, Toussaint's suspicion. Again and again, we were denied entry, and

---

[25] Alphonse de Beauchamp, qtd. in Korngold, Ralph. *Citizen Toussaint.* New York: Hill and Wang, 1963. Page xi.
[26] Beard, John Relly. *Toussaint L'Ouverture: A Biography and Autobiography.* Boston: James Redpath, 1863. Page 145.

spent days circling the island, composing letters attesting to our goodwill and receiving replies that hinted darkly at the possibility of engagement.

I began to entertain the notion that Toussaint, that dark-souled cheiftain[27], did indeed harbor secret ambitions on behalf of the slaves he commanded. Although I have blood sympathy with the African slave, an independent Hayti would be ruinous for the French Republic, as it remained the most profitable colony in the world under any nation.

On the fifth night of our circumambulation, Leclerc brought his generals together in the officers' quarters, under candlelight, and recommended that we call Toussaint's bluff and enter the city. "We cannot idle any longer in the ports of Saint-Domingue. It is my considered belief that we can both suppress the slave revolt here in Hayti, and proceed to Louisiana and lay claim to the French territories there."

---

[27] John Greenleaf Whittier, qtd in Beard, John Relly. *Toussaint L'Ouverture: A Biography and Autobiography.* Boston: James Redpath, 1863. Page 361.

This suggestion was met with silence, at first. "You will excuse me, General Leclerc, if I point out that in sending our navy into the city now, we expose ourselves to attack from every side." Ogé pretended disinterest, but he could hardly suppress the agitation which found expression in his hands, restlessly gripping and releasing the hilt of his sabre, safely tucked into its scabbard.

"But I have thought of that already, General Ogé. If we cannot storm Port-au-Prince in one swoop, we can sow the seeds of discord among the army and its leadership."

"These men, General," Ogé began, clearing his throat before proceeding. "Toussaint's men, they *sing* into battle. And it is not a marching song. They sing *for Toussaint*."

"Well then," said General Leclerc, folding his arms. "Since you are an expert on Toussaint, tell us why we should not attempt to turn his leadership against him."

Ogé leaned in close, and spoke raspily, as though he were an angler about to tell his best fish story:

"It may be strictly said that he is everywhere, and especially at the spot where sound judgment and danger would say that his presence is most essential; his great moderation, his power, peculiar to himself, of never needing rest; the advantage he has of being able to resume the labors of the cabinet after laborious journeys, of replying to a hundred letters every day, and of habitually fatiguing five secretaries; more still, the skill of amusing and deceiving everybody, carried even to deceit,—make him a man so superior to all around him that respect and submission go to the extent of fanaticism in a very great number of persons; it may be affirmed, that no man of the present day has acquired over an ignorant mass the boundless power obtained by General Toussaint over his brethren in Saint-Domingue; he is the absolute master of the island; and nothing can counteract his wishes."[28]

Quiet prevailed. The creaks in the wood from the shifting of our weight were audible in the ocean-silence.

"What do you suggest?" asked Leclerc. "Surely, you do not intend that we continue our somnambulations around this island, writing letters, enduring threats?"

---

[28] Vincent Ogé, qtd. in Beard, John Relly. *Toussaint L'Ouverture: A Biography and Autobiography.* Boston: James Redpath, 1863. Page 153.

"I intend that we swear to Toussaint, in writing, that if he helps us claim Louisiana, Hayti will have earned its freedom, and he and the rest of the slaves will be set free."

The next day, standing on a bluff of Mount Cahos were Toussaint, his officers Dessaline and Belair, Ogé, Leclerc, Rochambeau, and I. The vista afforded by the height was obscured by low-hanging clouds layering the sky as though to deceive us with a thousand false horizons. On a lower tree-covered promontory arose Toussaint's modest cabin, which had served as his family's retreat during the negotiations, appearing weather-beaten and strangely holy.

Leclerc, who was by temperament averse to asking favors, stood by diffidently. Ogé compensated for his superior's reticence with his tireless entreaties. It was his aim to avoid any miscommunication, to alleviate the Haytian's every doubt, to draw Toussaint into this pact inextricably; whereas General Leclerc and Rochambeau, in their barbarism, understood only the hum of war.

I watched Toussaint carefully, and decided that he was an uncanny reader of men. He knew precisely how to speak to each man so as to maximize the effect. Had he given Leclerc the mildest excuse, Rochambeau—Leclerc's mad dog—would have stolen Toussaint's children, ravished his wife, and marched France's armies over every surface of the island. And, looking finally upon Toussaint the man, I now understood, France still would have lost.

"It's a good thing that your navy was not here with the purpose of invading Port-au-Prince," said Toussaint to Leclerc, who raised his eyes to his addresser without lifting his chin. "It would have been a loss to Hayti *and* France if we had had to burn that city to the ground."

As we descended from the bluff, Toussaint spoke to me as though to an old friend. "If, at the end of this intrigue, I have the fortune of meeting with and addressing the Consul personally, I will be satisfied of its worth. I have always wished to speak with him, soldier to soldier, from the first among the blacks to the first among the whites."

"The Consul is less impressive in person," I warned Toussaint, as I walked him back toward the cabin. "His power resides all in his will. And in the imaginations of his enemies. In the physical world he appears . . . diminished."

"I am not easily deceived by appearances," he assured me.

Through Ogé's delicate diplomacy, Toussaint and Leclerc would lead the campaign into New Orleans together.

After the first salvo, the defending militia faded into the suburbs, effectively ceding the port to our navy. Intending to fight from the shadows, perhaps, like their neighbors the Indians, the people of New Orleans vacated their homes and took with them whatever they could carry on their backs, leaving the city corpse-still and ghost-quiet. Above the marching soldiers, laundry lines stretched from second-story windows, and beneath their feet, rats strode with renewed boldness.

Restless with the burden of a conqueror in an unfamiliar land, Leclerc sent all the French gendarmes through their drills, circling the city as a cat would claim its territory. Meanwhile Toussaint, with whom I travelled, commanded the Haytian soldiers to take after the New Orleanians into the woods. The jungles of the Louisiana Territory are dense and wet like those of Hayti, but the roots travelled aboveground, causing us to lift our legs high to trample thorns, and sometimes trip over skeins of bramble. The few men we spotted, we had to fire upon their backs as they took flight.

It became vividly clear that the shadow-war we were anticipating would never materialize. With the combined forces of the French navy and the Haytian army, there were more soldiers than citizens in all of Louisiana, so the city and its provisions would remain ours. So too would the rest of Louisiana Territory, the rightful property of France.

In the end, the East American States (then known as the "United States of America"), former colonies of Great Britain, bowed out of the fight honorably. As for the Republic of West Florida, east of New Orleans, soon the land was ceded to East America, and their government accepted this one concession as a victory.

Like the council on Saint-Domingue who had recently plotted his demise, Toussaint too had to wait in the stables while the Consul Bonaparte prepared for their meeting. But what was intended to evoke a sense of shame in the proud commander of Hayti's army instead comforted him with the familiar pungency of cavalry horses. Toussaint reminded himself that his personal fate was of little consequence. If the Consul fulfilled his promise of establishing an independent and free Hayti, there was no more that could be wished.

I was the Consul's footman on that day, partly out of a sense of duty to both parties, but mostly out of a curiosity that exceeded tact. I notified Toussaint that the Consul awaited his audience, and welcomed him into the palace. Napoleon stood at a conspicuous distance, arms folded behind his back, in full regalia. Despite my warnings, Toussaint was visibly chagrined, not by the man's stature, but by his petulant expression and faint air of boredom.

"Let's get to the quick," said Napoleon. "Both of us know that Hayti is a colony that depends on the labor of your men, and you know that Hayti cannot be made free."

"With every respect and due honor, sir, I know nothing of the sort. I know that the people of Hayti, as subjects of France, have fought alongside her army against the Spanish, the English, the Dutch, and the Portuguese, and that we have aided in the seizure of new colonies for the glory of the French Republic."

"And I hereby thank you on behalf of France," Napoleon remarked sarcastically, turning toward his advisors, who stood by with pinched smiles under their groomed mustaches. "Shall we raise funds for a statue?"

"Pardon my simplicity, Consul Bonaparte, but there was a treaty signed by your hand that promised a free Hayti, should its people prevail in the war on New Orleans, in the name of France."

"Ah, but there was no war," said Napoleon, feigning surprise. "They laid down their arms. And even if such a deal were made, you must have known that such a condition could never be accommodated." A moment of static silence. "Citizen Toussaint, my position is simple. Unless you and your kind are dealt with, *the sceptre of the New World will sooner or later pass into the hands of the Blacks.*[29] Your countrymen will never be free. Not in America, and not under the French Empire!"

---

[29] Napoleon Bonaparte, qtd in Korngold, Ralph.
Citizen Toussaint. New York: Hill and Wang, 1963. Page xi.

172

"Not yet," said Toussaint darkly.

"Excuse?" Napoleon said, not following the General's train of thought.

"France is *not yet* an empire. You are not an emperor."

I stepped away from General Toussaint when he spoke, as though he might instantly combust, such was the hold my brother-in-law had upon my mind. But rather, he stared coolly at the Consul, awaiting his unjust sentence, a living monument to *man's unconquerable mind.*[30]

The last time I saw Toussaint L'Ouverture, he was dressed in chains. A prisoner in the Chateau of Joux for nearly a year, a man forgotten by time and nature, he was like an abandoned soul in Dante's *Purgatorio.* There was a thinness to him that previously I had only thought possible in certain kinds of fish—where the bones are soft and flexible, and the flesh is silvery, the last vein of oil in his body beading up to the surface, waiting to be evaporated.

---

[30] William Wordsworth, qtd. in Beard, John Relly. *Toussaint L'Ouverture: A Biography and Autobiography*. Boston: James Redpath, 1863. Page 346.

I had not the heart to tell Toussaint how his champion Ogé had been banished to Elba, his former ally Leclerc killed in combat, and the barbaric Rochambeau appointed in his place. And most of all, I avoided any mention of the fate of Hayti, and any reference to what Rochambeau had wrought upon that land in his absence.

"Do you have regrets?" I said, speaking in the abstract to avoid giving voice to my own vivid regrets.

"Only that Consul Bonaparte does not keep his promises," he said.

Emperor Bonaparte, I did not correct him. "Do your guards give you no news?"

He shook his head. "As far as that, the world is silent."

"In that case," I said. "Let us say that Hayti is free."

I did not know it yet, but because Toussaint once lived, and because death cannot fully extinguish life of his proportion, Hayti *would* become free.

"I would call Toussaint 'a Napoleon,' but Napoleon made his way to empire over broken oaths and through a sea of blood. This man never broke his word. I would call him 'a Cromwell,' but Cromwell was only a soldier, and the state he founded went down with him into his grave. I would call him 'a Washington,' but the great Virginian held slaves. This man risked his empire rather than permit the slave-trade in the humblest village in his dominions."[31]

—

Thus was Louisiana claimed by France, and the architect of that victory betrayed and sentenced to slow death by the treacherous Napoleon. Yet, without General Toussaint's help, the victory in New Orleans, and consequently the fate of West America, would have been fatally compromised. Thus also was the question of slavery in the New World settled, West America established as a slaveholding property, and the seeds for the American wars sown, and grown into cotton, and sewed into a million uniforms, and soiled by the blood of a hundred thousand men.

---

[31] Wendell Phillips, qtd. in Beard, John Relly. *Toussaint L'Ouverture: A Biography and Autobiography*. Boston: James Redpath, 1863. Page 366.

CHAPTER 9:

Napoleon Invades Louisiana

Suggestions for Class Discussion:

Why did Toussaint believe that Napoleon would honor his promise to free the slaves of Haiti, France's most valuable colony? Why couldn't Napoleon tolerate an alliance with Toussaint? What would have become of the two Americas if Leclerc had gotten his way, and France, having depleted its navy on the Haytian rebellion, never showed up for the war in New Orleans? Who but Napoleon could have tamed the savage swamps of Louisiana?

Hitler Goes to Art School

A NEW THEORY AMONG ART HISTORIANS has emerged
that Adolf Hitler, a minor German painter (1889–1917),
had secretly aspired to a political career. Though the
trajectory of his life until 1914 clearly leads toward an
early death and a forgettable output of mediocre landscape
paintings (except for one notable painting of the Chancellor
Theobald von Bethmann Hollweg), this theory proposes
that, from his collected writings, we can determine that
Adolf Hitler was, in the delusional realm of his artist

studio, making plans for a political coup d'etat and a campaign of military conquest that would span all of Western Europe.

According to this theory, Hitler, unable to influence the aesthetic mode of his contemporaries in any appreciable way through his art, hoped instead to impose his artistic values upon the public through force. How he meant to achieve this goal is unknown, but the theme of his writings in the years 1914–17 offers some evidence to this claim.

The following text is written by August Kubizek, a friend of Adolf Hitler during the early years of his career, as a student at the Vienna Academy and beforehand.

—

So Herr Hitler would become an artist after all. If he failed to pass review a *second* time, Hitler was fond of saying, he would take his unholy vengeance upon us all. Though Herr Hitler was often given to dramatizing his anger.

Those first few months of his Academy training, Herr Hitler occupied himself exploring the streets of Vienna, where he gloomily watched street artists sell domestic art for a few marks each. He told me that there were only two kinds of paintings: those worth more than the frames in which they are set, and those that aren't. Until then, Hitler's own work had been used only to sell picture frames, but soon this sad state of things would change, he vowed.

Hitler began to meet with two of the Academy's professors, Herrs Schneider and Neumann. He seemed to avoid the students and faculty in general, preferring the company of old friends, such as myself. But Herr Hitler had chosen these artists as the most sympathetic to his ambitions. Herr Schneider found Herr Hitler's influence-jockeying detestable, and whenever he found the intense, dark-haired young man waiting at his office door, instead of taking him aside and issuing an impromptu lecture on Italian Renaissance painting, Schneider would simply invite him out for a drink. Upon learning that it would mean enduring the company of the other professors, Herr Hitler always declined, saying that he did not wish to mingle with charlatans and swindlers. He would rather shoot himself in the head, he said.

Herr Hitler was not shy of discussing his reasons. The dominant trend in the Academy during those years had been toward abstract expressionism, and toward representing inner landscapes without objective reality. Herr Hitler's expertise was in rendering monuments—vast structures that showed the scale of human achievement. His was an art of human ambition unbridled, explained Hitler, not of a bug's-eye view of the world, not "degenerate art," as he called it.

Herr Hitler was regularly passed over for grants and honors reserved for the most favored students of the Academy, but when Germany's Chancellor Hollweg came to Vienna and requested a capable student to paint his portrait for the Oktoberfest ("nothing *too* experimental," he said), Herr Schneider spat out Hitler's name. Schneider, though he disliked Hitler personally, was among those who, like Hitler, struggled impotently against the tide of abstraction in art. So it was that Herr Hitler would be the one honored with the duty of painting the Chancellor.

Through sheer force of personality, Herr Hitler had risen in esteem among a minority of faculty who regarded themselves as rearguard sophisticates. Not everyone was as receptive to Hitler's rhetoric—powerful though it was. The Rector, in particular, recoiled from Hitler's notion of art. The Rector declared to the committee that Hitler was simply unfit for painting. Hitler showed some skill as a draughtsman, maybe, and would excel in architectural drawing, but his renderings of nature—a popular subject— were, in the Rector's assessment, *unnatural*.

Herr Hitler found a sympathetic ear in Neumann—a boyish, bespectacled man much in the mold of Herr Hitler himself. It was Herr Neumann, in fact, who persuaded the selection committee to include Herr Hitler in the roster for this class of the Art Academy, and who told Hitler afterwards what a formidable antagonist he had in the Rector. Neumann knew instinctively how prone Herr Hitler was to irrational anger, and provoked him a bit, so I thought, for sport.

"Your renderings of nature are *unnatural*?" Herr Neumann said. "What can that mean? I suppose next the Rector will say that your lines are nonlinear and your shapes unshapely."

"Why would Austria allow such a man to preside over an institution like the Vienna Academy? How can *Germany* allow it?" Hitler said.

"Unfortunately, not everything is up to Germany."

"Germany is all. Have you ever noticed that anyone who matters is a German?" Herr Hitler said with confidence. "Austrians have become indulgent and weak."

Herr Neumann laughed and tilted back on his chair. "You are an ass. You should meet the Rector. *He*'s an ass. You'd like him."

Hitled frowned, unable to take anything lightly.

In the year 1912, winter arrived right on schedule, and Herr Hitler needed a new coat. His old workman's jacket was worn and ratty. Marching out into the cold, we took Vienna alley by alley, stopping in at coffee shops or pharmacies. Occasionally, we were mistaken for vagrants, and hustled out the door of a grocer's.

Near the Mannerheim, where the real vagrants slept, we saw two soldiers approaching from a rise in the sidewalk, one in his uniform, the other in plainclothes. At that angle, the three-story buildings seemed to tilt inwards and meet at the midpoint of the sky.

I mentioned this to Herr Hilter, though he, with his knowledge of perspective, pointed out that this was not the case—that the eye can trick the mind into seeing falsely.

"Hey, *vagabund*, why don't you come out of the cold, eh? Join the army," the soldier said. Herr Hitler paused and absorbed the image. A man with military posture, Nordic features, and golden hair. Cold blue eyes. Herr Hitler looked away, blushing.

"I'm not a vagrant; I'm a student," Herr Hitler answered. The plainclothesman offered him a smoke. Herr Hitler grimaced. "I just need a new coat."

"Well, look at this," the soldier said, holding onto his collar with both hands and loosening it, pulling outward to show the fabric inside. "Wool. Military issue."

"I'm not interested in a military career," Hitler insisted. I echoed his sentiment, and made as if to move along. This was, of course, before the war.

"Is that so?" The man leaned in uncomfortably close, as though for a kiss. "Then why are you still standing here?"

"Well, I'm not ungrateful. I wish I could serve my country as you do. But I'm just an artist, and no good at combat. Perhaps I could be useful in another way? I've always thought that I would make a good strategist."

The men looked at each other and laughed. "Well, here is where you start. Come follow us and we'll sign you up. Nobody becomes Napolean on his first day."

Just then, Hitler spotted Herr Neumann approach from the same hill. "I'm sorry, but I must excuse myself," Hitler said, and shuffled on so quickly that I was left behind momentarily, the central point from which the whole company dispersed.

I followed Herrs Hitler and Neumann to Ratsch's, the student pub. One characteristic that Herr Neumann didn't share with Herr Hitler was his abstinence. Herr Hitler was a notorious teetotaller, so sober that he tended to induce sobriety in others. While Herr Neumann, on the other hand, drank in a volume and intensity that was calculated to impress his colleagues and students. From what evidence I could gather, it did no such thing, but succeeded only in keeping his persistent sense of failure well-oiled.

When it came up in conversation that Herr Neumann and I shared an acquaintance from Salzburg, we paired off to chat while Hitler sulked alone by the vestibule, shuffling his feet as though preparing to dash back out into the cold at any second. For an hour or so he seemed to wait like a sentinel guarding the gates of a walled city, looking only occasionally in our direction, and when his eyes met my own, I swear they gleamed, flecks of orange dancing in the wet whites around his irises.

I was relieved when a man walked in from the street and immediately offered a seat to Herr Hitler. They fell easily into conversation, without much by way of introduction. I was surprised to see that Herr Hitler accepted a beer from the stranger, and seemed quite prepared to drink it, so I tapped Herr Neumann, who was facing away from the scene, and directed his attention to the spectacle behind him.

After smiling to himself for a long moment, Herr Neumann walked nonchalantly over to their table and nodded. "Herr Hitler," he said cordially, then turning to his companion, "Herr Rector."

Herr Hitler flushed red instantly. "Do you mean . . . ? This man . . . ?"

The Rector's eyes darted back and forth and he forced a smile in Herr Neumann's direction. "I see that my reputation is a larger canvas than the picture is worthy of."

Herr Neumann smiled his wicked smile back at the Rector. "Do you see, Herr Hitler, how even the Rector's meager reputation is now a 'canvas'? According to Herr Rector, art is everywhere, except in real things."

Facing the junior faculty member, the Rector recovered quickly. "Herr Neumann is developing a patent on reality, though I doubt anyone will bother to steal his design."

Curling his lip in disgust, Neumann tugged Hitler's shoulder and said, "Come, Herr Hitler, let's leave the expressionist to his little expressions."

When Herr Neumann saw that Hitler intended, instead, to sit and drink with the Rector, he sneered venomously at the pair. Both Neumann and Hitler, you see, lacked the ability to hide their contempt. They were German-Austrians, whereas the Rector had a dose of Englishman in him, and could hide his resentments easily.

Though Herr Neumann and I had been on our way to merry drunkenness, we had only just met, so I stayed with Hitler to satisfy my own curiosity. When Herr Neumann left the bar, it was the last we saw of him for a while.

"Tell me honestly, Herr Rector, what is it that you despise in my art?" Hitler asked.

"I don't despise it at all. You would be lucky to have an art critic despise your work. It would mean that it was deeply felt. No, I don't despise it. It simply lacks vitality." The Rector handled a book of matches indelicately.

"But you underestimate my ambition, and my capacity to grow as an artist. I have been painting three paintings a day for several months, and with each attempt my linework becomes more disciplined and my sense of composition more controlled."

"You are right; with every painting you grow in discipline and control." The Rector paused, on the verge of lighting a cigarette. "I do not judge the man, but I will gladly judge his work. You are no artist, Herr Hitler, but you have a true talent for architecture, which I hope you will have the sense to pursue."

"You know very well I don't have the degree required to go to *technic!*" Herr Hitler's voice took on a throaty vibrato that belied his sober state. "What does an academician know of art? All you know is bureaucracy and self-promotion!" It became clear to the Rector that any goodwill that seemed to exist between himself and Herr Hitler had been created solely to draw him out, to put him at ease enough to expose himself as Hitler's enemy.

Hitler threw his cap to the ground and stared *through* the Rector as if his point of focus were behind him, rendering the man invisible. "His face was livid, the mouth quite small, the lips almost white. But the eyes glittered. There was something sinister about them. As if all the hate of which he was capable lay in those glowing eyes."[32]

The day had come for Herr Hitler to paint Chancellor Hollweg in his office, and the Chancellor bustled into the room late, between meetings with Emperor Franz Joseph and his nephew Ferdinand. Their meeting was cordial, and Hitler sat straight down and began painting eagerly.

---

[32] Kubizek, August. *The Young Hitler I Knew.*

"Don't you need me to make a pose of some kind?" the Chancellor asked.

Herr Hitler paused, his eyes barely visible over the top of the canvas, his brows barely there and his hair angling wetly to the right. "Look like an emperor," he said.

The Chancellor, always fond of flattery, laughed. "I like that."

Though Herr Hitler often boasted of his speed as a painter, his portrait was taking longer than the Chancellor had the patience for. He had sat for photographers many times before, and never had to worry about his back muscles tightening, or his head feeling heavy on his shoulders. He broke pose, then strode across the room to look at the work-in-progress, so that his movements would appear purposeful rather than merely restless.

"Pardon my untrained criticism, young man, but this does not look right to me. The rendering captures a certain likeness, but overall the effect is . . . lifeless. You cannot see any of the inner animus that drives the human vessel. Do you know Carl Jung?"

Hitler kept his face neutral, except for his eyes, which

burned like pyres. "Pardon *me*, Herr Chancellor, but I am not painting your inner animus. I am painting your human vessel, and if you are unhappy with your human vessel, that is none of my concern."

The Chancellor laughed. "What insolence from a student!" he shouted, with apparent joy at the surprising disparity. "Nevertheless, start over, and this time I want you to capture my inner self."

"Why don't you understand that I am not painting your insides!" said Hitler, in a growling timbre for which he was famous among his friends.

The Chancellor's lips turned down under his gray Kaiser mustache, and Hitler's lips frowned back at him under his Chaplin one. "I suppose this will have to do," said the Chancellor, taking Hitler's unfinished painting from its easel and handing it off to a steward.

The resulting portrait, as I understand it, is Hitler's only notable work, mostly due to its subject, but also for the distinctly inhuman expression of the Chancellor. The composition places the head, oddly, toward the bottom of the canvas, and the rest of the room, in the space above, is rendered with architectural precision. But the face itself is done quickly and crudely. It is described as a sketch that an assassin might make of his next target.

After that day, Herr Hitler retreated into self-imposed exile. He rented an apartment far from the Academy, on Humboldtstrasse, not far from those domestic artists whom he had recently scorned. He attended classes seldomly, and when he did appear on campus it was ethereally, as a ghost might haunt an old building. His faith in art in the contemporary world had been cut away, somehow leaving his ambition intact, so that he went through life yearning and yearning with no hope of ever being satisfied.

In the summer of 1914, when the Archduke Franz Ferdinand was assassinated and the future of Austria thrown into doubt, Hitler left the Academy and signed up for the army, joining the ranks of the *Gefreiter*. From the letters I received from him over the next four years, I gather that he bored the other soldiers with his talk of a new Germany that embraced classical art and architecture, and refused the modern. I myself was a soldier in the

Austro-Hungarian Infantry Regiment, and had since met at least a dozen men like him—or *almost* like him. Theirs sounded like a clean and—with all its focus on monuments and other vast structures of stone—seemingly empty Germany.

The only account of Hitler's last moments comes from Friedrich Rader, a soldier in the 16th Bavarian Reserve Regiment, in which Hitler served and was eventually raised to the status of corporal. According to Rader's diary, Hitler was a lousy soldier, and did not make one notch on his rifle during the two years that he was deployed in Belgium. However, he did finally kill two Belgian foot soldiers when he lobbed a grenade over a bunker wall. Afterwards, as he entered the bombed-out bunker, Rader describes Hitler as a man full of *schiksal*, or "apprehensions of destiny." He stood in the center of the carnage, rapt in glory-feeling, with a palpable sense of the beauty inherent in dead things. He looked (though "look" is too slight a word in this instance) at the dead Belgians, with their insides turned out, and stood in awe at the chaotic red patterns on the wall.

—

Rader identifies this moment as Hitler's last. Kubizek speculates that Hitler was so in awe of the scene that he forgot that he was in a war zone, in Belgian territory, and was subsequently fired upon by enemy soldiers. In his last will and testament, Hitler had written, as though from the end of a long, prosperous career, that his paintings were intended "exclusively for the establishment of an art gallery in my native town of Linz. It is my heartfelt desire that this legacy be fulfilled."[33]

---

[33] Adolf Hitler, qtd. in Infield, Glenn B. *The Private Lives of Eva and Adolf.*

CHAPTER 10:

Hitler Goes to Art School

Suggestions for Class Discussion:

What evidence is there, from Kubizek's account, that Adolf Hitler would become anything other than a minor painter or architect? Why did Hitler himself believe that he could achieve anything but a modest living selling art for picture frames (see Figs. 3.3 and 3.4)? What did Hitler see as he stood enraptured at the center of that room full of dead Belgians? What do art and war have to do with each other?

Ho Chi Minh in Harlem

HO CHI MINH (1890–1969), grandfather to the frozen food industry, was born and raised in the Nghe An province of Vietnam, the son of a civil servant. Born Nguyen Sinh Cung, Nguyen took on the name Ho Chi Minh (or "He Who Enlightens") after moving to the United States. Ho began his American life as a pastry chef at Hotel Theresa in the year 1913, long before he began producing his specialty pastries as the first mass-market frozen food.

Ed Winston, an African-American prizefighter and a

lifelong friend of Ho's, asserted in his memoirs—excerpted below—that Ho had not intended to remain in the U.S., but planned to return to Vietnam and lead a revolt against the French colonial government. That he chose instead to become an American citizen and then an entrepreneur is a testament to the depth of his American idealism.

—

Ever since he returned from his tour of the heartland, Bac Ho wouldn't leave the neighborhood. When I asked him what he thought about America, he nodded his head thoughtfully and said, "America is fine . . . but Harlem is my home."

Three years ago, when he first arrived, all he talked about was returning to Vietnam—as soon as he learned the secret of how the Americans had cast off the yoke of imperialism to become the world's first free and independent colony. He came to America to learn the art of revolution. Then the *other* America got to him—the America of aborted plans and good intentions left out too long in the sun—and though he continued to speak of his grand scheme, his heart was not in it, and eventually he stopped referring to any other "home" than Harlem.

Bac Ho was the pastry chef in our hotel, the Theresa, and I was deli. Mornings we spent arm to arm, slaving away at the slicer we shared, alternating cheeses and meats, while residue formed in the selvedges like sludge. The kitchens are always the rearmost and out-of-the-way location in the building, where food can be prepared on the cheap, which at least put us next to the icebox, so that a summer wind through the windows actually brought with it a temporary coolness.

Early afternoons we passed orders up to the lunch counter, which appeared a model of efficiency as the servers swerved proudly between tables like salmon, wantonly depositing dishes on customers' tables like ovum in the gravel of a riverbed. But behind the scenes where we lived it was sort of a vaudeville performance, one that was so *avant-garde* it required no audience. Backstage, out of boredom, we scattered the dishes on the floor and lobbed food at them. We hung meat from the ceiling like lines of laundry and tenderized them with our fists, acting out the latest middleweight match-up (I was always Sam Langford KO'ing whichever white boy stood against him that week). We stuffed our guts with free food and held belching contests.

When he started at the Theresa, Bac Ho was so shy the staff called him "The Mute of Harlem." He had a child's habit of nodding his head when spoken to, but unlike a child, his eyes always met yours when he spoke. Whenever he stepped out onto the concrete, his head craned back and he'd stare at the jagged skyline of towers like they were ladies' legs opening above him. There was a bit of Chaplin in him, I thought, a foreigner's innocence and a contentment in rags.

In the late afternoon, when traffic slowed and the halls emptied, Bac Ho and I'd smoke a couple of torpedoes in the lobby, like captains of industry—and watch all the dames pass by on the street, as though we were window-shopping for a piece of kitty. And when a dame would eye us back? That was enough for a day's worth of talk.

Nights we spent choking down what was left from an

evening of restaurant service: we drank, literally, from the bottom of the barrel. The warm, foamy ale sloshed around the pails with the consistency and the vague smell of urine, but as it poured down our gullets, it had all the potency of mulled wine.

For a time, we were mere creatures of vice. Both of us holed up in the mess quarters like sailors on an endless loop of the world. In fact, that's exactly what Ho had done for years before arriving here: Paris, to London, to Marseilles, to Casablanca, to Boston . . . and New York. And the stories he told made me feel that I was a part of the journey.

They were good times, I'm soft enough to say. The trouble was that, between the two of us, there was no money. I could never save a nickel, and Bac Ho had just emptied his billfold in the heartland. Once in a while, I'd hear Bac Ho talk like he didn't need money, like it was no big deal, but then he'd get back to work earning his daily portion like the rest of us.

When I asked him what all his principles amounted to now, he'd just shrug and say, "A man's got to eat, hasn't he?" Three years in America, and Bac Ho was thinking like an American.

In France, Bac Ho had acquired a taste for cheese. Between all the American headcheese he was eating now, and his own talent for pastry-making, Bac Ho began showing some pink in his cheek. So that I could even imagine him breaking bread with the beer-bellied sons of Alabama. But when I pressed him on the trip, he said that in reality his sojourn into the heart of America had been like a fever dream. In Georgia, out in the western counties, Ho had been witness to a lynching, or so I gathered. His own report of the event was confused both by the trauma and the communication barrier. He tried to explain how they had burned a man, cut off his body parts, and then hanged him for good measure. But he couldn't get over the fact that the white men and women and children who filled the crowd were smiling, like guests at a Sunday barbeque.

"Do they enjoy suffering?" he asked.

On Saturdays our usual distraction was to train down to the winter garden to watch the Minsky's Burlesque. That night, I took Bac Ho out, gratis, as a sort of apology for the sad state our country was in. This was before Bac Ho told me how, in Vietnam, the French also executed the undesirables.

We were too late for seats, so we crowded out some kids for a close-up in the pit. In this particular classy production a young woman by the name of Baby Vamp came out first thing and showed off her strut, which looked a heck of a lot like a man imitating a woman's walk. She gave a speech celebrating certain foods which, through skillful innuendo, served to stand-in for the male anatomy. There were acrobats and jugglers next, and one clown came in and made a big show out of trying to ruin the act, but the acrobats and jugglers kept on going, and it turned out this joker was really part of the show, because then he joined in the tumbling and juggling like he hadn't ever realized that he'd been a master of the art all along. Later, Baby Vamp came back on stage as a coon shouter, cupping her hands around her painted-on big lips and calling out these zingers in what she must have thought was Negro-speak. Whatever it was, she made it look cute as all hell, and her country hat and nappy wig looked foolish on top of her small-featured face, even, as it was, stained black with shoe polish; so the whole thing was a gag, but when I turned my head there was Ho standing with his arms folded, stern as a wooden Indian.

The whole variety ended with a song, and since the cast was scarce they did a call and response to get the crowd going, and by the end nobody cared that they'd dropped two nickels just to make themselves look ridiculous. But the last act had ruined it for my pal Ho, so the walk home was quiet and made the city appear huge and anonymous, the way it did when you were new to it. "Shit, you'd think you'd just come from a funeral," I said, trying to cheer up the sour Oriental.

A few weeks passed before Ho brought up lynching again. "Forget about it," I said. "It's a terrible evil thing, I know, but what does it have to do with you? Was he kin to you?"

He paused, and turned his chin upward pensively, as if considering the possibility. Then he timidly extended his fist, which contained a crumpled pamphlet advertising a meeting of a group of Negro activists called the United Negro Improvement Association, which he must have found plastered to a wall in the slums. "I wish to go here," he said. "Would you come with me?"

I gave him a dodgy look, which meant I had no excuse but if he gave me time I could come up with one.

"I'll pay," he said.

"Whatever," I said, because if I didn't, then who would be there to save his ass if it got into trouble?

The UNIA met in a building not far from the Theresa. My own plan was to sneak in a pint of whiskey, sip it throughout all the speeches, and stumble home drunk. I meant no disrespect to my Negro brothers and sisters, but I saw in this new passion of his an implied threat to our idle nights and days, and was determined to undermine it. But what we encountered there was beyond my capacity to disrupt. Rather than an auditorium sparsely populated by dark-skinned men idling as they watched a parade of charismatic Negro intellectuals speechifying, it was not a stage at all, but more of a courtroom, where men and women in the crowd took turns making themselves heard.

There was a town-hall feel to it, as if here were the true voices of Harlem.

When the formal oratory had ended, and the scene devolved into an array of loosely related conversations, Ho made his way through the sea of dark faces toward the bench, where there sat a thoughtful and royal-looking Jamaican named Marcus Garvey, reminiscent of a lion in both the broadness of his face and the turned-down whiskers. Ho introduced himself as "a patriot from Vietnam," as though he were a man of importance in his home country. Throughout his introduction, Marcus maintained a respectful but aloof expression.

"There is something in your speech that I cannot understand," said Ho, the younger man, to his new mentor. "If you wish for there to be equality, how can you think of separating the races?"

Garvey smirked, visibly weary of this question. He turned to address me instead, saying, "Equality—the sort of equality your friend means—in America is an illusion. The struggle for equality is never about equality, but about power."

Ho spoke again, "Power, yes, but it seems to me that the real issue here is economic. If the Negro of America were to acquire wealth to rival the Caucasian, then they would enjoy the most real form of equality."

"Racial unity in the service of economic equality will never be a reality—not in this country," said Marcus, finally turning to address my Oriental friend. "But never mind that. Consider this: you are trying to remove the French from Vietnam?"

"Not so," said Ho. "We do not want to be ruled by the French, but neither do we want to remove them permanently."

"Because Vietnam is for the Vietnamese?"

"Of course," said Ho.

"Well, then Africa . . ." here he paused for effect, "is for the Africans."

Ho's face fell with disappointment. "I have heard a lyncher say that very thing."

"At least the lyncher is honest," said Marcus darkly. "Why did you come here? What does an Oriental care about the cause of the American Negro?"

If he was surprised by the question, Ho showed no sign of it. His eyes stared off into the distance as he recalled his childhood: "When I was thirteen years old, for the first time I heard the French words 'liberté,' 'egalité,' and 'fraternité.' At the time, I thought that all white people were French. Since a Frenchman had written those words, I wanted to become acquainted with French civilization to see what meaning lay in those words,"[34] Ho began. "When I learned about the American revolution, and the Civil War that abolished slavery, I wanted to understand what it means to be an American."

"Look around this room," said Marcus with a sweep of his arm that seemed to encompass all of the men and women of so many hues, unconsciously separated into discrete groups according to the lightness of their skin, "and you will understand what it means to be an American."

Then he added, "If you are looking for equality in America, then you may as well go home."

---

[34] Ho Chi Minh qtd. in Duiker, William J. *Ho Chi Minh*. New York: Hyperion, 2001. Page 45.

So Ho and I went home, to Harlem.

The lamplight outside the Theresa splayed out and fragmented as though seen through a cracked window. End-of-the-rain droplets tapped off-rhythm on the awning as we walked under it, into the lounge. Passing the other way through the mudroom, to our delight, was Baby Vamp, the new girl from Minsky's, her face streaked with the remains of what had recently been a painted face. There was barely enough space for the three of us in the glass foyer, so that we blocked one another's way, and stood on display for the saloon. Ho remained there, looking, in that piercing way that says he will not waver, he will not turn away. Baby showed, with a curl of her eyebrow, that she had the same way about her. I didn't need a coon shouter to tell me that it was time to make myself scarce and let nature take over, but after all the talk of politics, my head was hurting and I just needed to lie down on my own mattress. I motioned for the lady to pass, as I tugged at Ho's sleeve. She strutted past us, slow-like, smirkily twirling the end of her scarf.

Ho turned around to face her. "Excuse me," he said. "Please tell me your name."

"Mary Jane West, honey. Aren't you adorable."

To that, he replied with the same unwavering look. "And are you a guest here at the hotel?" he asked.

"That depends on whether I'm invited," she said suggestively.

"My name is Ho. I am a dessert chef here at the Theresa; if you should ever need something sweet, please ask after me, and I will take care of you."

That night I spilled into sleep as soon as we reached the room, while Ho stayed up smoking the rest of his pinch with a pipe, listening to the fading storm through an open window. I half-woke in the middle of the night to the sound of a gentle rapping on the door. A muffled Brooklyn voice from behind the door called, "Hurry up. You make *me* wait, and I'm gonna make *you* wait."

In the morning, Ms. West stuck around, strutting about the room in her way, casually nude, like a Frenchie. She picked up a photo of a younger Ho standing by the doors of his high school in Huê. "So where did you say you were from again?"

"Vietnam. It's near China," he said.

"Yeah, I own a map," she said, then added with a smirk. "Now I can check that one off the list."

"I thought for a long time I would return, but now it becomes hard."

Mae winked. "I know it does." She picked through her purse for a brush. "So how'd the likes of you end up in Harlem?"

"I work for a shipping company, so I've been all over the world, but I come here to learn how to free Vietnam."

"Well, aren't you the patriot?" she said. "I've been all over the world too, but the only thing I ever set free was a fella." Now she was moving the brush through her hair, tenderly, as though it were a separate animal. She caught me staring and shifted slowly, draping a sheet over her shoulder in a show of modesty which, under the circumstances, appeared comically coy. "So when did you give all that up?" She reclined in the bed, so that her upper back pressed against Ho's chest familiarly.

"The statue of Lincoln in Union Square," he said. "When I first saw it." In response, Ms. West raised an eyebrow and cocked her head to the side to give Ho a view of her in profile. He continued: "There he was, a humble man, a man of modest tastes and means, turned into a god by history. If I ever did go back and free Vietnam, I realized, someday I would be made a statue too, and the blind worship of our flawed heroes would go on." He paused. "Even in America, our leaders are untouchable."

"Oh, they're touchable, all right; take my word," said Ms. West, springing forward in the bed and doing an about-face to look at him directly. "If you want to change the world, baby, go find the President—just walk right up to Woody Willie, shake his hand and say, 'listen, me and you have got a date with destiny.' Know what I mean?" Ho wore that distant look again."At least that's how I'd do it," she said, standing up to dress at last. "But, hey, to each his own."

In the center of Hanoi there is a lake called Hoan Kiem, the "Lake of the Returned Sword." At the center, there is

Turtle Tower, which commemorates the legend of King Le Loi, who, like King Arthur, received a sword imbued with divine powers from the bowels of the lake, in order to fulfill his destiny and triumph in war. And like Arthur, Le Loi was told that once his war was ended, he was to return the sword to the lake from whence it came.

This is how Ho answered when I asked him how he could, as a victim of French imperialism, spend his days cooking French pastries. "Don't you *hate* the French?" I asked. We were at the slicer again, and he was cutting off pieces of cheddar.

"No," he answered, surprised at the suggestion. "I admire the French. Once we have run their armies out of Vietnam, we will invite them back as guests. And the sword will be put away."

"You may as well put away the sword now," I said, thinking that my friend Ho, lost in his old dreams of glory, needed a rude awakening, "and take up the cheese knife. Because the French are there to stay. And this, right here," I gestured to include the food, the stoves, and the whole hot kitchen, "is the American Dream."

Ho stopped slicing momentarily, and the break in rhythm was punctuated by the sound of clinking glasses in the front kitchen. "You are right," he said, resuming the action of the knife, looking down at the mess of color on his apron, which puffed out slightly with the new weight he had borne since becoming an American. "If there ever was another dream than this, I've already forgotten it."

—

It was not until the 1950s that Ho's real coup took place: Uncle Ho's Ready-Bake Frozen Dough. With his natural ingenuity and canny business sense, Ho Chi Minh was able to capitalize on the broad accessibility of the refrigerator by selling the first oven-ready dessert pastries to the mass-market. His early dabbling in radical causes eventually made him a target of the House Un-American Activities Committee and a personal project of J. Edgar Hoover's, but through his persistence Ho overcame these setbacks to become one of the richest and most influential men in America.

In marketing pre-frozen items, Ho revolutionized the food industry and ushered in a new era of packaging and distributing edible goods. Soon after Uncle Ho's Ready-Bake Frozen Dough changed the way we buy and sell pastry, other food companies followed, domino-fashion, with their own frozen food lines. And America's grocery stores have never been the same.

CHAPTER 11:

Ho Chi Minh in Harlem

Suggestions for Class Discussion:

In light of Winston's memoir, did Ho's decision to stay in America represent a sacrifice of principles? If so, what was Ho giving up by remaining in the United States? Ho Chi Minh was, at a very young age, determined to do good in the world; would you consider his impact on American food to be primarily a positive or a negative one? Which is the greater glory: food or politics?

CHAPTER 12

Einstein Saves Hiroshima

ALBERT EINSTEIN (1879–1955), theoretical physicist and discoverer of the theory of relativity, played a curious role in the failed Manhattan Project (1940–1945). Soon after his sixtieth birthday, while working at Princeton University, he was visited by former student Leó Szilárd (1898–1964), who had been conducting groundbreaking research on nuclear chain reactions based, in part, upon Einstein's own physical research. Szilárd approached Einstein with the proposition that they compose a letter warning President

Roosevelt of the possibility of Germany developing nuclear weapons. Knowing this would mean the government would be compelled to develop nuclear weapons of its own, Einstein demurred. Anticipating heinous future acts of war featuring unfathomable civilian casualties, Einstein regarded it as his duty to not contribute to the development of those weapons.

The following excerpt concerns the intersection of the lives of Albert Einstein and Leó Szilárd, and what Szilárd regarded as his former teacher's failure to support his cause. The article was originally written in 1959 by Szilárd, to explain the disappointing conclusion of his work at the Manhattan Project.

—

Einstein couldn't write his name. He had the intention, but not the will. He got so close as to hold the pen, poised shakily, over the letter, which I had written to warn President Roosevelt of the possibility of developing a doomsday weapon that could wipe out a city with a single drop. I knew, though, that it would never be heeded unless it came with the authority of Einstein, the leading scientist of our generation.

I stood in Dr. Einstein's office, on the top floor of the Institute for Advanced Study, near a window overlooking the pine forest. Young trees, that's what I noticed. Different from a Hungarian forest, as American things were always different from Hungarian things. Not so impressive, those trees, except for the rust-colored floor of the forest, from all the dead pine needles that had been sent down over their small years; brighter even than autumn's orange.

It was August of 1939, on the cusp of the season, and the very molecules in the air were agitated. As I waited for him to sign, I opened my mouth as if to speak, then thought better of it. I would never say it, but I thought it: *Would it be easier, Einstein, if you were not German?*

"I am sorry, Leó. I must hold out hope that we can defeat the Nazis without such a weapon, which would bring me nightmares for the rest of my life," Einstein said, putting down the pen, and offering a signature rise of the eyebrow.

"But the world knows you, Albert. What can I do? What can I do with this terrible knowledge, that such a weapon is made possible by science that *I* developed?" I appealed to his sense of common purpose, as a fellow scientist.

He closed his eyes, then, and bent his head. He put the pen back in its holder. "Leó, my friend," said Einstein. "Now you know what it is to have a monster."

In 1905, when Einstein was twenty-six years old, he discovered the equation for mass-energy equivalence. This is the version of the story as told to me by Einstein himself:

Sitting at his desk at the patent office in Bern, Albert Einstein stared, squinting, at the plaster wall. Somewhere, a superhuman was pursuing a renegade beam of light, almost catching it, but falling back, and then, at such a speed, held up a mirror to see what was reflected. *What did he see?* Albert wanted to know. No one could answer him; and few even cared to take up the exercise for mental sport.

The riddle was no different from dozens of others that Albert had asked himself over the years, during his idle moments, except that he could not leave it. It was like a toy soldier he had picked up as a child, which he'd been handling for so long that it had become a household idol.

Weeks, months passed in contemplation, and Albert found no peace from it. Looking up then from his reverie, Albert noticed that all of his coworkers had gone home, and the sun was about to set outside his west-facing window. *Where had Michele gone off to?* He wanted to ask him about this puzzle; he knew nothing would come of it, but it would make for stirring conversation. He stood up, slid on his jacket, and left the office, heading to the house of his friend Michele Besso.

He arrived at Michele's home after dark, in the cool of May. He walked in with barely any attempt at a greeting, eschewed small talk, and went immediately into his imagined scenario, this favorite thought experiment. What would the lightspeed superhuman see who, in his vanity, attempts to admire his own face in the mirror? Would the pace at which the light reflects off his face distort the picture? Would he appear farther behind than he really is, because of the speed at which he is moving? Would he see glimpses of the recent past, his reflection calling forward to him from history? Or would he see nothing at all? The two men volleyed notions back and forth like tennis balls, but the question remained stubbornly unresolved.

As it grew late, the possibility of discovering the solution, and the significance of that solution in proportion to their exhaustion, was narrowing. The answer, Einstein supposed, must wait for another lifetime. Meanwhile the question would have to endure.

On the way home by streetcar, however, Einstein happened to catch, out of the corner of his eye, the clock tower. He concentered all his thought on that clock, and the streetcar in which he rode, accelerating away at not-quite light speed; the clock, the car; the turning of the hands, the tires wheeling into the distance. He projected himself in the place of the clock, where time moves at exactly the pace of the hands on its face. Then, he watched himself soaring off into the distance, turning back to see, not a mirror, but a clock face slowing down, stopping entirely, as the light it emitted failed to reach his lightspeed body.

The next day, Einstein again intruded on the solitude of

his friend Michele, this time by brashly announcing, "Thank you, I've completely solved the problem."[35]

"Oh, yes? Is there a solution?" Michele had just gotten into his workclothes, and had a sheen of wet on his hair, and a fresh look to him. He was amused by the sudden appearance of the dishevelled genius at his door.

Einstein slouched into the armchair in the foyer, which most days we used as a place to lay old coats and wet umbrellas. "An analysis of the concept of time was my solution. Time cannot be absolutely defined, and there is an inseparable relation between time and signal velocity."[36]

Michele's first reaction was to smirk. "So in order to answer your riddle, you have to do away with time altogether . . ." And just like that, Michele understood implicitly the catastrophic depths of this revelation.

When Einstein told me of the moment when he first discovered the constant speed of light, it's relationship to mass, and the extraordinary amount of energy that could be

---

[35] Albert Einstein, qtd. in Feinstein, Jonathan. *The Nature of Creative Development*. Page 324.

[36] Albert Einstein, qtd. in Isaacson, Walter. *Einstein: His Life and Universe*. Page 123.

produced by a small amount of matter, he claimed that he had no inkling of its potential for being used for bombs. But when Einstein came to the home of his colleague Michele Besso that evening, and explained what would become his greatest revelation, I imagine that Michele, the more practical of the two, sighed a sigh so wide and deep it could have swallowed us all.

Einstein's monster, I knew, could not remain caged for long. So I proceeded without the help of Albert, and without the full support and funding of the White House. I was given a small office in Manhattan, which implied without a doubt that they had no expectation of my success. From my liaison in Washington I learned that the War Department had taken to jeeringly referring to my small operation in an office building on the Lower East Side as "the Manhattan Project," a title which I appropriated in a moment of quixotic pride.

I was able to acquire a staff, but no matter how steadfastly we worked, we were too small, our resources too meagre, to conduct substantial research on nuclear fission, a new direction in physics and one demanding the attention of the greatest scientific minds of our time.

Though Einstein had not lent his name to my cause, he visited our office on occasion. He had been my teacher in Berlin, so if I were prone to flattery I might have chalked it up to his admiration of my research. But I could not help but wonder why this great man would take the train all the way from Princeton every couple of weeks, just to visit one of many of his former students. In retrospect, it is clear to me that Einstein did not come by our lab to give his blessing to this birth, but rather, knowing *it* would be born no matter what, wished at least to babysit his monster.

That a functional doomsday weapon could be built in five years, from conception to prototype, I realize, was preposterous to begin with. By 1944, Germany had been defeated, and the Nazis were far behind us in research, despite having a great deal more resources devoted to the development of these weapons. Yet I could not abandon the Manhattan Project. I was inspired by the story of Einstein's discovery of mass-energy equivalence, and now that Maleva had passed away, she could not add, "Yes, Einstein's perserverence paid off in the end; but in the meantime, oh, how miserable he made all of those around him!"

We were both Ahab; the difference was that Einstein, when he set out on the ink-black sea, knew not what monster he had been pursuing. I knew exactly the markings on the white whale; could recognize its every scar; but I could not spear it with the tools I had—too blunt and flimsy to do anything but provoke the beast.

Years later, from a conversation with Niels Bohr (one of the few physicists who would still associate with the disgraced scientist I'd become), I learned that Einstein believed that such a weapon would be developed in his lifetime. He had written to Niels that, "When the war is over, then there will be in all countries a pursuit of secret war preparations with technological means which will lead inevitably to preventative wars and to destruction even more terrible than the present destruction of life."[37]

---

[37] Albert Einstein, qtd in Clark, Ronald. *Einstein: The Life and Times.* Page 698.

How humbling, how innocent it seems to me now, for my former mentor to believe that *I* could build a weapon so devastating as to change the nature of war itself.

When Roosevelt died, there was no time in our office for mourning. Truman took office, and the timeline for the Manhattan Project rapidly accelerated. My charges and I went from being tucked away and forgotten by the government, to being told, on a surprisingly cool late-summer day, when the fans were still turning, but to no purpose, "It is time." There would be no test run, and there was only enough uranium to build a single prototype. The President wanted it to be dropped on the enemy, and the war ended decisively.

Against my better judgement, and against the vow of secrecy I had made to the President himself, I sought to consult Einstein on this fatal step. I found myself once again at the Institute for Advanced Study in Princeton, a supplicant at the doorway of genius. This time I endured no wait, I suffered no disappointment. He grabbed his suit coat and ushered me out of the office; I followed him to the pine forest, where he padded down to what appeared to be his favorite path, worn to the dirt.

At first, he said nothing. Deeper into the woods, the trees were older; some of them older than the man walking beside me. There was a rope bridge overhanging a brook, such as you could see all over the mid-Atlantic states in the middle decades of the Twentieth Century, now completely overlain by concrete. Then, before stepping onto the bridge, he turned toward me and said, "Don't, Leó."

How he knew what I was about to tell him, I can only guess. Perhaps he had connections in the War Department. Perhaps he was a spy for Russia (he had, at one time, been a member of several Communist groups). Or perhaps he simply had an intuitive sense of the narrative of science; that one thing leads to another, and that it all ends with a great entropic emptying into the void.

"It is not up to me, Albert," I confessed. "It is an order given by President Truman himself that the atomic bomb is to be tested on the city of Hiroshima."

Einstein sunk lower into his collar than before, as though a chill wind had just passed over us. "President

Roosevelt would have forbidden the atomic bombing of Hiroshima, were he alive."[38]

"*Were he alive*," I said. "But there's no use in such speculation. We have to deal with the conditions we have *here and now*."

"But the conditions we have here and now are unthinkable, Leó. Science does not belong to us—I cannot fault you for pursuing the knowledge. But to *use* this knowledge . . . " Even when inveighing, Einstein used a flat, rational tone. "Science does not belong to us, but neither do the lives of men and women, to snuff out at our convenience."

"Would you then oppose the bombing of Japan?" I asked, testing my own resolve, my indignation at any trace of doubt that what I was about to do was the right thing.

"I will always condemn the use of the atomic bomb against Japan."[39] He took a step forward, onto the bridge.

I could not help but notice that, as he walked shakily

---

[38] "Einstein Deplores Use of Atom Bomb." *New York Times*. 19 Aug. 1946. Page 1.

[39] Otto Nathan & Heinz Norden, eds. "Einstein on Peace." Page 589.

along the boards of the rope bridge, he spoke about it as though it had already taken place, as though there was nothing to be done. Despite lacking absolute existence, the persistence of time could be a persuasive force.

The slogan for the mission was "no surprises." So much could go wrong. A crash, a lightning strike, an electrical outing, a false discharge. Any number of triggers might have detonated the charge, and left us a pinch of ash in the urn of history. By our very nearness to the beast, we risked our destruction.

The Enola Gay, the B-29 Superfortress, had been selected personally by Colonel Paul Tibbets, who would fly the bomb over Hiroshima. In her wake, there would follow another B-29, called Necessary Evil, which would photograph and document the event for science. Because I had spent so much of my life in development of the science behind the creation, I wanted to be present for its birth. I refused outright to deliver the plans for the bomb unless I was guaranteed a spot on the Necessary Evil.

It was a risky move, to make such demands, and it

caused me grief later on, as a Senate committee questioned my intentions in withholding the blueprint and my loyalties as a citizen. But the great wingless bird was about to leave its nest, and all the mother can do is watch and pray it takes flight.

Before taking off, I joined in the last-minute inspection of the bomb. A simple projectile; I was struck again by its deceptive ordinariness. *With one fatal drop of this teardrop-shaped steel structure*, I remember thinking, *man will finally have wounded God.*

A few of the boys had drawn obscene pictures on the side of the MK1, which they code-named "Little Boy," with the same spirit of smug cheer in which an athlete might name his largest teammate "Tiny." A more puritan mind might have considered this profane, as though a dirty picture of a naked woman diminished the austerity of the act. But, to me, the influence of the woman upon the bomb was not nearly so ugly as the influence of the bomb upon the woman, and it was the nuclear heat pulsing like a restless demon from within it that despoiled those crude lines, which were, by comparison, divine.

The hatch opened with a pneumatic hiss. The launching device lowered and aimed. Little Boy slid out. The dragon's tail tilted down. The demon egg dove and tumbled, and tumbled and dove.

In the city of Hiroshima, word had already reached many of the people of a bombing raid on its way, though no one could say precisely *when*. And then, as the shadow of Enola Gay passed over the paper buildings, I had the sensation of holding a match to a model city, igniting the curiosity of a boy unappeased by his imagination only; who needs to *feel* the fire in order to believe in its heat.

The men and women of Hiroshima had been bombed before, and the more jaded of them simply went about their business, indifferent to the threats. So that, when Little Boy touched down, there was a small crowd gathered around the crash site.

It was supposed to detonate before touching the ground. But after a moment, nothing. Enola Gay and the Necessary Evil circled like vultures, flying lower when it became clear there would be no detonation, the camera still rolling.

It landed, *thud*, in Edo Street near the Imperial Gardens, but not before passing through a high-arching tree, throwing peach blossoms down in a slow-falling aftermath. No boom, no blast, no gust. Little Boy's crash-landing cracked the street beneath it, rolling ever so slightly, then settling.

A young girl in school uniform, an elderly man carrying fishing gear, an amorous couple still dressed in last night's wrinkled eveningwear, a city official halting his frantic gesturing, all stopped to gather and stare at the monolith. Some people backed away, or ran, or hid behind what shelter they could find, but a few of the spectators to the scene moved in on the object, slowly. The schoolgirl reached out her arm, and touched the metal with the flesh of her forefinger, and didn't draw it back until her nerves had time to report back its heat.

Would it be unfair to them to say that they looked like apes staring upon a UFO? Very well then, I am unfair. But when it comes to Einstein's monster, we are *all* apes looking on, fascinated and confused, waiting to see what will happen.

—

When Szilárd learned of the failure of the bomb to discharge, and to create the chain reaction necessary to cause the destruction of Hiroshima, as he tells it, his first thought was, in a word, "Einstein!" But despite volumes of FBI data on the elderly German physicist, there is nothing to directly suggest that he was anything but a humble man of science; his resumé was not that of a saboteur.

Yet the failure of the Manhattan Project was the beginning of the end for nuclear research. After Japan's surrender, the allied powers determined that nuclear technology was unstable and unpredictable. The science for building such a bomb was theoretically sound, but in the frenzy to end the war, the United States had nearly committed a sin of global scale, and used its misfire to make a public denouncement of doomsday technology. The Truman Doctrine, articulated only a few years after the failed mission of the Enola Gay, held that all nations must work together to prevent the development of nuclear weapons by any individual nation, a policy which will remain in place as long as human society can suppress its inclination toward self-ruin.

CHAPTER 12:

Einstein Saves Hiroshima

Suggestions for Class Discussion:

If Szilárd *had* gotten Einstein's support, the Manhattan Project had been fully supported, and the Enola Gay's mission had been completed successfully, would the United States be seen differently throughout the world? If Einstein anticipated Szilárd's innovations in nuclear chain reactions, would he have withheld his own groundbreaking scientific research? Does the scientist have any responsibility to the greater humanity, or is his obligation to progress only?

The Coronation of King George

EVERY GENERATION BELIEVES that the whole of history culminates in *them*: *their* conflicts, *their* tragedies, *their* follies and triumphs. But we were the first to feel that history was behind us—not leading *to* us, but terminating *before* us, so that in our post-history haze we would have sailed on toward any utopia, Aquarius or Xanadu, rather than stare back in the face of the mare. Yet history canters on indifferent to its load, and far from staring in its face, we remounted and rode upon it for decades to come. Until an unprecedented attack on home soil brought our utopian vision shaking to its knees; until George, son of George, rose from the dust fields and oil fields of old Mexico to answer history's beckon and declare an end to fear itself; and we were uplifted by the noble hand of our future king.

Our king! Yes, every other generation had believed that the whole of history culminated in *them*. But now we could not help but feel it too, as we saw the crowning of our first king, on every station, on every computer monitor, in every classroom. The technology we used to watch was already half a century old, but when we saw the King of America coronated, in the year 2004, we knew then what the media was for. These days, it is hard to remember what we did with all those screens before our king was declared. Watch shows about fictional people doing fictional things? Check in with the "news" about the lives of ordinary people?

Those faint pleasures were like memories of childhood, a time both innocent and vaguely disturbing. That we could *be there* with him! That we could *be* him! *That* was the magic of the screen.

The moment was, and is, indescribable. It was as though something we had secretly yearned for, but did not yet know that we yearned for, were suddenly offered to us, and both the temptation and the satisfaction were laid at our feet in the same moment. If you've ever bought a weekly tabloid at the grocer's, paging through it to find the latest dalliance of the European royal families, envious at the beauty and extravagance of their foreign monarchies; if you've ever stared into a movie screen at a parade of Hollywood icons, like a pantheon of gods, and wanted that smugness to be your own; if you've ever known the thrill of offering yourself up totally to an indifferent lover, enduring every shame with a smile; then you know the libidinous joy it gave us all to watch our country put for the first time in the hands of a single monarch.

The Europeans had had a long history of kings, and treated the news with blasé skepticism. The pundits whispered "figurehead" whenever the name King George was uttered, because they all had come to think of kings and queens as sock puppets performing theater for the amusement of the people (in whom the power of government was truly vested). But *our* King George was different. He was not ridiculous; he was heroic. And his power was real.

The offer, if it were to be binding, had to be made by his political adversaries. Otherwise, it would appear as though the gesture lacked unity or consensus. This was easy to arrange, as there was no serious dissent among the patriotic men and women of the 108th Congress. How could there be? King George, in his years as president, had been right about everything; every whim, every estimation, every assumption of his was borne out by its result. He correctly guessed that a Middle Eastern dictatorship had been collaborating with terrorists in a plot to deliver nuclear weapons to our doorstep. He devised the foolproof strategy of launching an awesome missile attack in its most populous city, then training the former militants of that dictatorship to suppress budding insurgencies. He understood that, by sweeping away their tyrant leader, we had gained their trust, and would be welcomed with open arms by the whole country (our liberation and subsequent control of the country being the sole issue upon which all factions could agree), as we were.

His successes were so numerous and assured that the mildest murmur of doubt among his detractors sounded to all like the vestiges of a pre-Georgian negativity. And the cornerstone of his foreign policy, preemption and surveillance, was applied equally to domestic affairs, so that his opponents found it expedient not to depart too stridently from the consensus view, embodied in the person of the president. "The President is the People," the party had taken to saying, and though this had irked certain members of the opposition for its galling contradictions, it was close enough to reality (the President was studiously "of the People") that his people-like demeanor eventually won over even the cosmopolitans of New York and the brahmins of Massachusetts.

So it was his chief opponent, at one point a contender for the presidency himself, who was appointed the honor of offering the crown to the President. This was after the President's latest triumph: privatizing local and state government. When George had moved to privatize Social

Security, there was an initial hesitation, followed by a mood of uncertainty, which was ultimately dispelled by the President's common-sense reasoning: "Let the people keep their own money" was his mantra, and if the citizens of the country felt it in their wallets, there was little to interfere with progress. When the administration successfully privatized the prison system, the efficiency and directness of the business model seemed to have won out.

With rampant bureaucracies at all levels of government, it was only a matter of time before the President took aim at bloated local and state governments. Critics called it "the new feudalism," but the rejoinder was as eloquent as it was effective: "The only one around here who seems to want to 'feud' is *you*," said the President. Soon, the moniker sprang back at his opponents and stuck: critics of the privatization of government were henceforth branded "the new feudalists," for their propensity to feud with the President.

The first offering of the crown was staged at a bill-signing in Virginia, within a hundred miles of the White House, where he returned and issued a statement through his spokesman that afternoon, stating his reasons for declining the historic offer. The strong-chinned, oval-headed vaguely ethnic-looking man in glasses read monotonously into the podium microphone: "The President is humbled and flattered by the call from the citizens for him to assume the mantle of king. However, any gesture toward a single-party government cannot be taken seriously at this time, and would be irresponsible so soon before a national election."

The White House followed the second offering of the crown with a longer delay, before ultimately reaching the same verdict. This took place on Martha's Vinyard, after a historic treaty-signing between Israeli and Palestinian leaders (which feat the President too had arranged on his off-hours). The same bespectacled spokesperson, with his becalming presence, offered more rational equivocations. "While the President believes that a strong executive branch is essential to good government, he feels that the current system has served the United States adequately. Though the elaborate system of checks and balances built into the Constitution may be outdated, the members of the Congress and Senate do provide an invaluable service."

The final offering of the crown, as has been immortalized in story and song, took place in the most appropriate setting for a President whose most lasting legacy had been reforming the military and boosting its morale through quick and clean operations abroad: aboard an aircraft carrier. This was soon after the 2004 election, notable as both "the first electronic election," conducted and compiled entirely through digital means, and "the last election in America," for its clear mandate for the President's "declaration of freedom": to proclaim the United States liberated from terror and confusion.

The Vice President stood at his right side, with the Speaker and members of the opposition to his left. A photograph of the King, in his last moments as President, shows a crowd of old men behind him—bejowled and steel-eyed, coiffed and costumed in a manner befitting their station. As for the President, the only flourish on his traditional navy suit and red tie was a gold cummerbund and upturned collar. This slight variation on a theme gave the scene an attitude more regal than stately.

The anointed stepped up to the podium, squinting into

the camera, and through the camera, into the eyes of every man, woman, and child in America. He pursed his lips tightly, in his way, as though tasting something sour.

"I accept this responsibility, bestowed upon me by the American people and our esteemed representatives, in order to strengthen and unify the nation in a time of increasing bureaucracy and confusion from within, and increasing threat from without. As President, I must acknowledge the widely held view among our people that, as a nation, our choices are few—do we remain with the status quo and let government run like business as usual, or do we forge ahead in a new direction for the nation, and the world? The answer, all agree, is to become the pioneers of history, to trailblaze a path toward efficiency in government for the world to follow."

The nation emitted a collective sigh, so long and ardent that it seemed to hiss out of the land like air from a punctured tire.

There were a few factional groups outside Washington that caused a stir. The state of Vermont even started a movement to secede, but that inconsequential cheese wedge of a state did not even go so far as to form an army. They spent weeks writing letters and signing petitions, then their energy fizzled. *How do you know*, the secessionists asked, *that this is what Americans want*? But the only proof they needed was the apathy of the republic. What sign would you ever need, other than silence?

When the weather started to change—when a great hurricane struck the Gulf Coast and emptied it of its largest city, the contents of the city literally spilling into the ocean with the tide; when the tornadoes ravaged the Midwest, leaving mile-wide scars on the land, like frustrated children stomping on their playthings; when the earth opened up under our neighbors' cities and took whole buildings with it into the sinkhole; when oil rigs failed, pitiful and powerless to plug the hole with its black plumes, spilling their veins into the ocean like Marat in his bloody bathtub—King George gave the only consolation he could: that this, as everything before and after it, was just God's work. And this was enough! The nation observed a moment of silence. Candles were lit. Money poured in

When the sun began to burn the naked skin of men, when glaciers melted and the sea level rose, when the dust storms returned, King George came to rely on the Book of Revelations, and the apocalyptic glory found there. He did not come out and say "rapture," as there were still many contrary religions in America in the Twenty-First Century, but you could see it in his way of holding his arms aloft, preacher-like, and bringing them down on the podium, like the hands of God on the sinner.

The weather! Our King's bane! He'd been right about *everything*. Why wouldn't the weather fall in line? If reality is perception, as the court upheld, what prevented nature itself from adhering to the beliefs of himself and his people?

Industry was not to blame. Industry only implemented what science had wrought. Science had *discovered* the problem, so why wasn't science doing anything to *cure* the problem. Indeed, by developing the technologies that lead to waste, wasn't science the original *cause* of the problem? And, King George took pains to ask, are we even sure that it *is* a problem, except that "science" says so?

King George always managed to bring the larger issues down to a manageable size. "Back in my hometown, we always used to say, 'He who smelt it, dealt it,' and I believe that to be the case in this instance." In other words, science had *identified* the problem, and now it was science's responsibility to *clean up* the problem.

But science, like terror, like freedom, like God, was not a nation, or a person, to be blamed, or cajoled, or waged war upon, and it simply stood by, monitoring the patterns of the storm as it churned around us, the circle ever narrowing to include our neighbors, but we the living always confidently standing in the eye of the hurricane.

When NASA leaked that new technology made Mars a real candidate for habitability, it was once again science—science!—and not politics, which took center stage in the world theater. All the talk was of "terra-forming," and "ecosynthesis," and most galling of all, "international alliance." It was the specter of international dependence that caused the King's men to marshall their forces and launch their ambitious mission.

Suddenly, technology was the new savior, and King George risked becoming the next great American irrelevancy. But if you knew the King, you know that he could never allow someone's faulty notion of progress to make him into another old news story. So King George announced a bold new plan for the future of America, and the world: to launch ourselves into outer space. Starting with the King and his royal retinue. He held a press conference to declare his intention to become, along with his retinue, the first colonists of "New Earth."

"New Earth" would begin a new story, a new episode in the history of man, a new front in the war on weather. Most of all, it was—as the King was overheard saying through a live mic—"just another fucking frontier."

At first many believed that, by taking off for another planet, he was giving up on this one: as though he were admitting that the earth was despoiled beyond hope. Some of those who had begun to despair asked, *What happened to the captain going down with the ship?* But what we, in our innocence, had forgotten was that the King is a man who lives by glorious example. He propelled himself into space, not because it was the only way to escape the impossible predicament in which he found himself as king, but because he wanted to show us that *we too* could escape the world someday, as he did. We could never envy his plunge into the void, as it gave us some distant star to which we could all aspire.

During the press conference, in answer to the question of whether it is possible to govern from such a vast distance, the King stood loose-limbed and bobbed his neck like a rooster before the fight, put on his best cowboy face and said, "I'll be back."

He stood on the platform leading to the shuttle, stopping to wave at the ocean of men and women who had come to see him off. He rested his hand on the corrugated steel shell that lined the walkway. It made a warping sound that, though entirely standard for its construction, made all of us in his vicinity wonder at the flimsiness of this entire enterprise. That the machine was vulnerable to the King's touch made us all feel helpless. The millions cheered and cried and held high the flag of the Empire.

As he settled into the cockpit—a feature strictly

unnecessary to the shuttle's design but made exactly to his own specifications, bone-white and body-sized like a bathtub—the King regarded himself in a convex mirror. He had aged suddenly, Lear-like, and everyone in the kingdom had noticed. His eyes were eyes that took everything in view and reduced it to a pinpoint of light that glinted from the corner of his pale iris; when faced with its bulbous reflection, the eyes squinted into nothing, as though the mirror gave off a painful light. Yet he could not look away. His impulses were unimpeachable, even if they launched him into the void and left a chewed-up earth behind. It was fitting that the King should wander off into the woods like an old wolf, rather than die upon a rug like a hound.

His favorite gadgets were arrayed behind him, none of which kept pace with the latest technology: a mercury compass, a gas mask, aviation goggles, control panel with neon-green digits on the screen. There was a cassette tape player, currently halfway through the B-side of a Learning Chinese language tape. The bathtub itself was suspended by bundled copper cords that would serve no useful purpose once it reached zero gravity, and frayed slightly as the King rocked from side to side, gripping the yoke of the steering column. In the unlikely possibility that he encountered lifeforms, the King carried a Rubik's Cube in his pocket, as testament to man's ingenuity.

When the shuttle launched, there was a feeling common to all watching, that it was not our King launching into outer space—that it was the world, and us, falling away from him. Like children watching our father pull away in a station wagon, going around the block, but never emerging on the other side. It was the revelation that, He *did* leave us, *didn't* he?

And he is out there still, floating farther and farther toward a tiny speck in the distance that will grow larger with time. And though from the outside he may look like a senile Quixote in a pod drifting deeper into cold and empty space with no glimmer of life in sight, the reality (which is perception), is that the King of America is just another confused and hungry soul seeking salvation someplace far, far away.

Acknowledgments

When it comes to the writing of this book, there are more thank-yous than breaths. First, I owe a great debt to all of my family, friends, and colleagues who have supported my writing habit, especially Emily & Hien Nguyen, and Dorothy & James Hershman. But I want to pause here to imbue this written appreciation with deep significance, given how easy praise can be in our Age of Affirmation.

For the individuals named in the Acknowledgments of my first book, *Memory Sickness*, you are doubly thanked. A third round of thanks are due to Trudy Lewis, Deb Brenegan, Rose Marie Kinder, Stephen McCabe, Bayard Godsave, and Kevin Prufer, for reading this book in its development and encouraging its fulfillment.

A big wasabi-chunk of thanks goes to Sarah—without whom this book never could have been written—and to Toby, Henry, and Ben.

The new thank-yous:

To Erin Knowles McKnight, editor of Queen's Ferry Press, who willed this book into existence with her time, energy, and enthusiasm; to Kate, Brian, Lulie, and all of our Warrensburg friends, for your good company; to Ben Johnson, for becoming a scholar of alternate-history; to Alexander Weinstein, for building a workshop in utopia; to Art Ozias, for opening his doors each morning; to Mike Rush, for the animated book trailer; to Daniel Mollenkamp, for the live-action book trailer; to An Quigley, for photography and website design; to Cole Dillingham, audiobook sound engineer; to Brian Reed, for advice on all things technical; and to Gersham Nelson, for his daily service.

For your ongoing support and encouragement, I thank B.J. Best, Tom Williams, Garry Craig Powell, Michael Martone, Rachel Raimist, Rob Arnold, Marcus Wicker, Dan Chaon, Joseph Haske, Ken Chen, Zachary Mason, Michael Nye, Thomas F. Dillingham, Shawn Setaro, Allison Joseph, Jon Tribble, Michael Kardos, Catherine Pierce, Matt Bell, Tiphanie Yanique, Travis Kurkowski, B.J. Hollars, Allyson Godlin Loomis, Karissa Chen, David Baker, Zhanna Vaynberg, E.C. Osondu, Maryfrances Wagner, Michael Czyzniejewski, Jen Murvin, and Christine Sneed.

With great appreciation for Mark Halliday and Jill Rosser, who discovered "The Great Pyre of Egypt" for *New Ohio Review*; Frederick Barthelme and Travis Kurowski, who found "Siddhartha Remains in His Father's Palace" a good fit for *Mississippi Review*; and the people at *North American Review* for welcoming "Joan of Arc, Patron Saint of Mothers." Thanks to Rusty Barnes, who picked up "John Smith Is Hanged for Treason" for *Night Train*; Richard Burgin, who took "Hitler Goes to Art School" for *Boulevard*; Thom Bassett, who seized upon "Plato, King of Syracuse" for *Bryant Literary Journal*; Marc Watkins, who found a use for "Einstein Saves Hiroshima" in *Front Porch Journal*; Lydia Ship and Anna Schachner for making "Benjamin Franklin, Clergyman" welcome at *Chattahoochee Review*; Paul Ruffin, who secured "Ho Chi Minh in Harlem" for *Texas Review*; David Hamilton, longtime editor of *Iowa Review*, whom I've never had the fortune to meet, but who had the foresight to pick up the story that would eventually lead to this collection: "Columbus Discovers Asia"; and to Elise Capron, who discovered poor Columbus lost in the streets of Shanghai within the pages of *Iowa Review*, and urged me to write this book.

Photo by An Quigley

PHONG NGUYEN is editor of *Pleiades* and author of *Memory Sickness and Other Stories*. He directs the Unsung Masters Series, for which he edited the volume, *Nancy Hale: On the Life and Work of a Lost American Master*. Nguyen teaches fiction and American literature at the University of Central Missouri, where he lives with his wife, the artist Sarah Nguyen, and their three children.

CPSIA information can be obtained at www.ICGtesting.com
Printed in the USA
BVOW00*1554020214

343548BV00001B/1/P

9 781938 466236